The
Integration
of
Mary-Larkin
Thornhill

The Integration of Mary-Larkin Thornhill

ANN WALDRON

E. P. Dutton
New York

The publisher and author gratefully acknowledge permission to quote from the following poems:

Page 62: " 'We Real Cool'—The Pool Players. Seven at the Golden Shovel," from *The World of Gwendolyn Brooks* (1971) by Gwendolyn Brooks. Copyright © 1959 by Gwendolyn Brooks. Reprinted by permission of Harper & Row, Publishers, Inc.

Page 104: "Amazing Grace—How Sweet the Sound," from the Presbyterian *Hymnbook.* Published by The Westminster Press.

Page 110: "Camera," from *Stars and Atoms Have No Size* by A. M. Sullivan. Published in 1946 by E. P. Dutton & Co., Inc. Reprinted by permission of A. M. Sullivan.

LIBRARY OF CONGRESS CATALOGING IN PUBLICATION DATA

Waldron, Ann   The integration of Mary-Larkin Thornhill

SUMMARY: School integration brings many changes to the life of a southern girl as she enters junior high.

[1. School integration—Fiction]   I. Title.
PZ7.W1465In   [Fic]   75-15505   ISBN 0-525-32580-8

Published simultaneously in Canada by Clarke, Irwin & Company Limited, Toronto and Vancouver

Designed by Meri Shardin
Printed in the U.S.A.
10 9 8 7 6 5 4 3

For Thomas William Waldron

Chapter 1

"I guess we'll move," Missy said.

"What do you mean?" Mary-Larkin asked.

"You know. . . ." Missy stopped. She was sitting crosslegged on a quilt spread out on the flat roof of the porch of Mary-Larkin Thornhill's house, and she was bending her neck as she squeezed a lemon into her hair. She rolled her head so the lemon juice would go all over her scalp.

Mary-Larkin was stretched on her back, eyes closed, soaking in the summer sunshine.

"What?" Mary-Larkin asked. She liked to have everything spelled out.

"You know—" Missy said again. "The school and all."

"Oh." Mary-Larkin sighed. "Integration." She had forgotten about integration.

"Won't your folks move?" Missy asked.

"We can't," Mary-Larkin said.

"That's right," Missy said.

Mary-Larkin's father was a Presbyterian minister and

1

the Thornhills lived in the manse, the house the church furnished them, so they had no choice about where they lived.

"We wouldn't move if we could—you know that," Mary-Larkin said.

"Well, we may not have it," Missy said. "Integration, I mean."

Mary-Larkin said nothing. Of course, we're going to have it, stupid, she thought. Don't you read the papers? Don't you know anything that happens in the world? Missy never read anything if she could help it. Then she pushed these disloyal thoughts away. She and Missy had known each other ever since they could remember, in Sunday school and through six grades at Millie Bybee Elementary School. And Missy was one of the most popular girls in the whole town of Stonewall.

Mary-Larkin opened her eyes to look at Missy. "Your hair is really getting light," she said.

Missy had been sitting in the sun all summer, squeezing lemons into her long, light-brown hair, and it now had lots of blonde streaks in it.

Mary-Larkin's hair was dark brown and curly and lemon juice had no effect on it whatsoever, except to make it so sticky it had to be washed. She hated it.

"If we could just go swimming," Missy said.

"I know," Mary-Larkin said.

"It's your mother's fault," Missy said.

"No it's not," Mary-Larkin said.

Early in the summer, some black children had tried to swim in the Stonewall public swimming pool, which had been for whites only ever since it had been built. The

Stonewall City Council had simply closed down the pool. It stayed closed, while lawsuits were filed. The summer got hotter, but the pool stayed closed.

"My mother just asked them to open the pool again," Mary-Larkin said. "She just went down to the city council meeting and asked them to open the pool and let *everybody* swim in it."

"Well, it sure caused a fuss," Missy said.

"It sure did." Mary-Larkin had to admit that Mrs. Thornhill had caused a big fuss. Her picture had been in the *Stonewall Independent* and she had gotten anonymous telephone calls and unsigned letters telling her she was a threat to the white race and the American way of life.

Missy's mother had looked pityingly at Mary-Larkin at the time of the big Swimming Pool Crisis and hugged her. As though somebody had died, Mary-Larkin thought, remembering.

"Mother says we may build our own swimming pool," Missy said.

Mary-Larkin was pulled back to the present and the sunny porch roof. "Oh, great," she said.

"Will your mother let you come over and swim in it?" Missy asked. "If we do build one?"

"Sure," Mary-Larkin said. But she wasn't all that sure, to tell the truth. Her family had really made a big deal out of that city Swimming Pool Crisis. Mr. Thornhill, at family prayers the morning Mrs. Thornhill's picture was in the paper, had prayed for God to keep them strong to stand on principle, to listen to the voice of the Holy Spirit instead of the voice of the crowd.

3

Missy's family never had family prayers and never talked about the Holy Spirit as though he were a *cousin*, the way Mary-Larkin's family did, and Missy's mother had never been to a city council meeting in her life.

Some of Mary-Larkin's friends' families had joined the country club so they could go swimming, but Mary-Larkin's family had flatly refused to consider it.

"The country club excludes people," Mrs. Thornhill had said. And she had turned back to her typewriter.

"What are you writing now?" Mary-Larkin had said. "Some more old Sunday school stuff?"

"Some more Sunday school stuff," Mrs. Thornhill had said as she pecked away.

"Aaaaaaaugh," Mary-Larkin had said.

Mrs. Thornhill had laughed and gone on typing.

Mary-Larkin pretended to hate her mother's "Sunday school stuff," but she was really pretty proud of her mother. Her mother wrote the pupils' books for Sunday school classes in every Presbyterian church across the South. That was better than anything Missy's mother ever did, wasn't it? Or was it? Mrs. Cobb arranged the flowers in the church and—well, she shopped a lot.

"Oh, listen!" Missy said. She turned up the little radio on the quilt beside her and the music flooded the rooftop like the sunshine.

"When I'm down and feeling low. . . ."

Both girls were quiet. Missy tapped her fingers to the rhythm.

When "Like a Bridge over Troubled Waters" was over, Missy suggested they practice cheerleading.

They both got up, and stood poised, side by side, hands

4

on hips, and left toes pointed out. "Let's do, 'Hit 'em a lick,' " Missy said, and Mary-Larkin nodded.

Moving in unison, they rolled their arms; they knelt; they leaped at the climax, leading an invisible stadium full of junior high school football fans in an earth-shaking roar: "Yea, Longstreet!"

Then they collapsed on the quilt. "We're getting good," Missy said. "Maybe we'll both get to be cheer-leaders at Longstreet."

She reached over and turned the radio up.

"And now we bring you this bulletin," an announcer was saying. "The Fifth Circuit Court of Appeals has handed down a decision in the Stonewall desegregation suit. The Court has set new boundary lines for attendance zones for each school. Superintendent of Schools Ralph Wilson says he will comment after he has had time to study the plan. Maps showing the new school zones will be posted in the Board of Education offices by tomorrow, Wilson said. The N.A.A.C.P. filed suit in the Federal courts. . . ."

"Integration is here," Mary-Larkin said.

Chapter 2

"We're in the Phyllis Wheatley district!" Missy told Mary-Larkin over the telephone the next morning. "My mother went down to the school board and looked at the maps."

"But that's a black junior high, isn't it?" Mary-Larkin asked.

"Yes, it is," Missy said. "And my mother says we're definitely going to move."

"What about Callie and Sarah and Grace Will Byrd?" Mary-Larkin asked, naming off their best friends at Millie Bybee Elementary School. "Are they in the Wheatley zone, too?"

Missy wasn't sure.

"Let's go look ourselves," Mary-Larkin said. "We can ride our bikes."

They pedaled downtown to the school offices and looked at the maps posted in the corridor. There was a big crowd milling around, with people peering at the maps and then gasping or screaming or laughing with relief, as they found their own school districts.

Mary-Larkin and Missy tunneled through the crowd to

the junior high map. Avondale, the area where they lived, was an older residential area near downtown, and it had all been zoned into Phyllis Wheatley.

Most of Magnolia Gardens, the residential area of new houses just beyond Avondale, was still in the Longstreet district, the junior high Mary-Larkin and Missy had expected to attend.

"Look, Jessie Adams is safe," Missy said. (Safe meant she was in Longstreet.)

"And Grace Will is, too," Mary-Larkin said.

"Sarah Knox and Callie Hubbard are in Wheatley," Missy said.

"What about the boys?" Mary-Larkin said, trying to remember which block Noble Paget lived in.

"Steve Smith and Bill Lawson are safe," Missy was saying.

"Bruce Davenport and Monk Stevens and Noble Paget are in Wheatley," Mary-Larkin said. Her heart leaped with joy at the thought of Noble Paget, who had held her hand on the playground at Millie Bybee.

They picked out the zone for nearly all the thirty members of their sixth-grade class at Millie Bybee, and then they moved over to the senior high map.

"Avondale is in the Carver district, too!" Missy moaned. "That awful nigra senior high."

"Ssssh," said Mary-Larkin, looking around her nervously.

"It means if we don't move we won't get to go to Robert E. Lee," Missy said. Robert E. Lee was the best high school in the state, everybody agreed. The Lee football team always won the state championship and the drama students always won all the prizes at speech

7

tournaments. Lee always had more National Merit scholars than any other high school in the state, and its graduates—at least lots of them—got into Harvard and Yale and Randolph-Macon.

"Gosh," said Mary-Larkin.

They moved slowly over to the elementary school map.

"We're still in Bybee," said Missy, pointing to her block on the map.

"We're not," said Mary-Larkin. "We're in some school I didn't even know was there. I can't read the name of it. . . ." She peered at the map and finally made out the words, Crispus Attucks.

"Joe and Luke will have to go to Crispus Attucks," she said. Joe and Luke were her younger brothers, ten and eight.

"Let's go," said Missy, and they left, bicycling back home through quiet streets, not talking.

"See you," Mary-Larkin said when Missy turned off to go home.

Mary-Larkin put her bicycle in the garage and went in the house. Her mother was upstairs typing. She looked up when Mary-Larkin came in.

"Mama, we've been down to the school board. We're in the Phyllis Wheatley district!"

"Oh, really?"

"Mama, I don't want to go to Wheatley."

"You'll like it once you get there," Mrs. Thornhill said.

"Mama, I want to go to Longstreet."

"Well, you can't, if you're in the Wheatley district."

Mary-Larkin left. No use talking to her mother.

That night at supper, Mary-Larkin's father asked the

blessing and served the plates and passed them around the table.

Joe and Luke sat on one side of the table and, as usual, began to eat without talking. Mr. Thornhill asked them what they had done that day.

"We went fishing out at Possum Creek," Joe said. Joe, two years older than Luke, usually did the talking.

"Did you catch anything?"

"No, sir," Joe said.

"They never catch anything," Mary-Larkin said.

"They will some day," Mr. Thornhill said. "And what about you, Mary-Larkin? What did you do today?"

"I went to the school board office and looked at the maps. We're all zoned into new schools."

"New schools?" Even Luke looked up at this. "What do you mean?" Luke had blue eyes and blond hair, the only blond hair in the Thornhill family, and he hated school with all his heart. He lived for Saturday morning and cartoons on television.

"You two have to go to Crispus Attucks," Mary-Larkin said, getting a certain satisfaction out of their startled looks.

"Crispus Attucks? Where's that?" Joe was frowning and peering at Mary-Larkin through his glasses.

"It's over in Spanishtown," Mary-Larkin said.

"Spanishtown?"

Spanishtown was an old quarter of Stonewall where a great many of the town's black people lived. Nobody knew where it had gotten its romantic name.

"Crispus Attucks?" Joe asked again.

"It's a black elementary school, dummy," Mary-Larkin said. "It's integration."

9

"Oh, integration." Joe turned back to his plate. He had lost interest. Integration had been about to happen so long, Joe seemed to feel he could wait a little longer to see what really was going to happen.

"I have to go to Phyllis Wheatley," Mary-Larkin said.

"That's a black junior high, isn't it?" Mr. Thornhill said.

"Yes, sir, I don't want to go."

"Why not, Mary-Larkin?" her father asked.

"I want to go to Longstreet," Mary-Larkin said. "Where all my friends are going to go."

"All your friends can't be going to Longstreet," Mr. Thornhill said. "We certainly can't be the only white family assigned to Phyllis Wheatley."

"Jessie Adams and Grace Will Byrd are both still in Longstreet," Mary-Larkin said.

"What about Missy?" Mrs. Thornhill asked.

"Their house is in the Wheatley district," Mary-Larkin said. "But her family was talking about moving even before the court order. She said she was sure they'd move now."

"Oh, they wouldn't leave their nice old house just to avoid going to an integrated school," Mrs. Thornhill said.

"Wait and see," said Mary-Larkin. "I bet they *do* move."

"Who else is in the Wheatley district?" asked her mother.

"Sarah Knox and Callie Hubbard and Mell Stockton," Mary-Larkin said. "Bruce Davenport and Monk Stevens and Noble Paget."

"See," Mrs. Thornhill said. "You'll have lots of friends in Wheatley."

"And you can make new friends," Mr. Thornhill said. "It will be good for you to know some black young people. When I was growing up in Wildflower, Mississippi, I played with black children all the time. Of course, I don't mean that life was fine back then—the situation was unjust. But at least, I did get to know some black people. Nowadays white children don't know black people at all, not even as servants. My family was poor, but we had a cook and two maids."

"We see Booker," said Joe.

"We don't see Booker near enough," Mrs. Thornhill said, and everybody laughed. Booker was the handyman in the Avondale section, and he was so busy you had to ask him months ahead to do something.

"Integration is a good thing," Mr. Thornhill said in the voice that Mary-Larkin always thought of as his preachery voice. It was the voice he used in the pulpit or when he talked to anyone about Good and Evil. It was a serious voice. "We have treated our black brothers unjustly and we must make amends. There may be a little friction as we begin to make changes. But we must remember that sometimes there can't be light without heat. We must all work together and learn to live together in Love and Brotherhood."

It sounded like a sermon, Mary-Larkin thought. We might as well eat supper in church, she thought. But Papa was right. That was the trouble—Papa was always right.

Mary-Larkin sighed so loud it sounded like a tornado.

11

Chapter 3

"We bought a new house!" Missy told Mary-Larkin over the phone the next day.

Mary-Larkin felt as though she'd been hit in the stomach. She couldn't even breathe for a minute.

"Where?" she asked.

"Magnolia Gardens," Missy said. "Wait until you see it."

"Come on over," said Mary-Larkin.

When Missy arrived, they got Cokes and Ritz crackers and took them out on the front porch. They sat in the rocking chairs on the shady porch that smelled of Confederate jasmine that climbed the posts and twined around the railing.

"Where is it exactly?" Mary-Larkin asked.

"It's on Gardenia Street and it's brand new."

"When did you all buy it?"

"Yesterday," said Missy. "Mama went out and looked the day the ruling came down, and she took Daddy out to see it that night. They bought it yesterday—they didn't even tell me where they were going. It was a real surprise!"

"Won't you miss your nice old house?" Mary-Larkin asked.

"Yeah, I will," Missy said slowly. She looked sad for a minute, and then she tossed her streaky head and looked at Mary-Larkin. "I just couldn't go to school with Negroes, Mary-Larkin. Mama said we just weren't raised that way. We're Southerners through and through, and Mama said we just couldn't mix with Negroes."

"We're Southerners through and through, too," Mary-Larkin said. "Papa grew up in Wildflower, Mississippi, and Mama is from Jackson."

"But your folks are—" Missy stopped. She had started to say "Your folks are crazy," and Mary-Larkin sensed it. Missy finished up, "Your folks are different."

Mary-Larkin was still feeling as though she'd been hit. She had occasionally felt that she'd like to have a more congenial best friend than Missy Cobb, but now the thought of losing Missy's companionship at school was terrifying. "My folks are different, all right," she said.

"Are you *really* going to Phyllis Wheatley?" Missy asked.

"I guess so," Mary-Larkin said.

"Well, I'm not," Missy said. "Our new house has a little attic and Daddy says he's going to fix that up for me, for a little sitting room. Won't that be neat? I'm going to have studio couches instead of beds and a TV and a stereo up there. . . ."

Missy chattered on and Mary-Larkin listened.

When Missy left, Mary-Larkin went to find her mother.

"Mama, let's drive out and look at the Cobbs' new house," she said.

"So they really bought a new house, did they?" Mrs. Thornhill said. She got up from behind her typewriter and said, "If you can find the car keys, I'll go."

Mary-Larkin started downstairs to look for the car keys, a familiar chore. When I grow up, Mary-Larkin thought, I'm going to always know where my car keys are. And I hope I don't have to wear glasses, because Mama is always looking for her glasses, too. Please God don't make me have to wear glasses and don't make me go to Phyllis Wheatley school. . . .

They drove out to Magnolia Gardens and turned off on Gardenia Street and found the Cobbs' house. It was brick and one story with a tiny attic.

"It's not near as nice as their house in Avondale," Mrs. Thornhill said.

"It's new, though," Mary-Larkin said.

"What's Mrs. Cobb going to do with all those antiques?" Mrs. Thornhill said.

"I don't know," Mary-Larkin said. "But I really like old houses best. I'd hate to move out here."

"Of course you wouldn't want to move to Magnolia Gardens," Mrs. Thornhill said. "You know what's right, don't you?"

"Oh, Mama, is everything a question of right and wrong?"

"Sure it is," Mrs. Thornhill said.

When they got home, Mary-Larkin looked at the manse as though she'd never seen it before. It was old, way over a hundred years old. It had been built in 1847, the year the church had been built. It was big, with high ceilings, wide porches, extravagant halls, and tall windows with

14

wavy panes of glass. Like the church building next door, it bore an historic marker.

Mary-Larkin loved it. She liked the wide, bare boards in the front hall, the acanthus leaves carved in the woodwork in the front rooms, the plaster medallions in the ceilings.

She didn't mind that it only had one bathroom—and that was made out of a bedroom. She didn't mind that it had no closets, just wardrobes.

The Thornhills had been in Stonewall for eight years, and Mary-Larkin could barely remember life in any other place besides the Stonewall manse.

Slowly, she went inside and helped her mother fix lunch. She went outside and yelled for Joe and Luke, who were playing some mysterious game in the alley behind the church.

After lunch, she called Sarah Knox and Callie Hubbard and Mell Stockton, who were supposed to go to Wheatley.

"I don't know what we're going to do," Sarah said, "but my father doesn't want me to go to Phyllis Wheatley. He's afraid I'll get raped."

Callie didn't expect to go to Wheatley, either. "My mother's afraid I'll get behind in my schoolwork," she said.

Mell Stockton was out of town.

Mary-Larkin went to tell her mother about Callie and Sarah.

"My goodness," said Mrs. Thornhill. "I thought the Knoxes and the Hubbards had more sense."

That night, Mary-Larkin heard her mother and father

talking over the school situation for a long time.

"We'll just have to provide some moral leadership," Mr. Thornhill said.

Mrs. Thornhill told Mary-Larkin not to worry. "We're going to have a meeting of parents here so we can talk about the Wheatley situation, the whole situation in the Avondale section."

"Did you call Mrs. Knox and Mrs. Hubbard?" Mary-Larkin asked.

"We did," Mrs. Thornhill said, "and the Cobbs and the Smiths and the Davenports and the Kingsleys and the Stevenses and Mrs. Paget. We called all the parents whose children have been zoned into Wheatley school. Maybe we can help people overcome their fears."

"There's no use asking the Cobbs," Mary-Larkin said. "They've already bought a new house."

"They haven't closed yet," Mrs. Thornhill said. "Maybe they'll reconsider."

Mary-Larkin genuinely admired her parents, although she seldom admitted it. This time, though, she thought, they've bitten off more than they can chew.

Chapter 4

The night of the parents' meeting, Mary-Larkin helped her mother get out cups and saucers for coffee, and she put Mrs. Thornhill's ice-box cookies on a plate.

"How many ice-box cookies do you make a month?" Mary-Larkin asked.

"One million," said Mrs. Thornhill. "I discovered right after we got our first church that it was like money in the bank to have ice-box cookies in the freezer. I make them every week, early in the morning before you're even up."

"If you can always have ice-box cookies on hand, why can't you ever find your car keys?" Mary-Larkin asked.

"I guess I think it's more important to have ice-box cookies in the house—oh, I don't know, Mary-Larkin!"

The doorbell rang. The first parents were there. It was the Kingsleys.

"How do you do?" Mary-Larkin said. "Come in. Have a seat."

She didn't know the Kingsleys very well. They went to the Unitarian church. All she knew was they were Stone-

17

wall's biggest liberals. They flew the United Nations flag on UN Day and they were the backbone of the Stonewall chapter, American Civil Liberties Union.

They ran a furniture store and decorating business, and, everyone agreed, it was a pretty elegant furniture store for a town of a hundred thousand people like Stonewall.

The Kingsleys had two children. Their daughter was the older and she was in college and engaged to a boy from Taiwan. The other child was a boy Mary-Larkin's age, Critter. His real name was Crichton Kingsley, but he had been known as Critter as long as anyone could remember.

Critter was the messiest boy in Stonewall. His shoe-laces were always untied, and usually broken, if not missing altogether. If he wore loafers, the soles came un-sewed. His shirttail always came untucked, and the buttons popped off his shirt spontaneously. His jeans ripped while he was standing still, and his hair was usually in his eyes.

Mary-Larkin was glad Critter hadn't come with his parents. She led the Kingsleys into the living room, and the doorbell rang again. She went back to the front door and opened it. Two young women stood there.

"Hello," Mary-Larkin said. "Come in. I'm Mary-Larkin Thornhill."

"I'm Edna Jo Reeves and this is Linda Bowling," said the tallest of the two. "We teach at Wheatley Junior High."

Mary-Larkin was leading them across the hall when Mrs. Thornhill came hurrying from the kitchen.

"Oh, Miss Reeves and Miss Bowling! I'm so glad you

could make it," Mrs. Thornhill said. "I'm Janie Thornhill and this is Mary-Larkin, who will be a seventh-grader at Wheatley."

"We've already met," Miss Reeves said, smiling at Mary-Larkin.

Mrs. Thornhill led them into the living room and introduced them to the Kingsleys. The Kingsleys immediately began to ask questions about Wheatley.

"How long have you taught at Wheatley?" "How is the discipline?"

"We taught there just one year," Miss Reeves said.

"Discipline was *terrible* last year," said Miss Bowling, the short, blonde teacher. "But there's going to be a new principal, and I hear he's very good."

The teachers sat down on the sofa and looked earnestly at Mr. and Mrs. Kingsley. "You know it will be so wonderful to have parental support," Miss Bowling said. "This is a great idea—to have a meeting."

"Were you assigned to Wheatley?" Mrs. Kingsley asked.

"No, we *asked* for a black school," Miss Bowling said.

"We *wanted* to be in a ghetto situation," Miss Reeves said.

"But of course a truly integrated school will be even more interesting," Miss Bowling said.

The doorbell rang again, and Mary-Larkin went back to her duties. Mr. and Mrs. Knox, Sarah's parents, were at the door.

The Knoxes went to the Presbyterian church and Mary-Larkin knew them well. "Where's Sarah?" she asked. "Why didn't she come?"

"We thought she'd better stay home," Mr. Knox said.

Mr. Knox was in the real estate business, and Mrs. Knox worked in his office.

"Are you coming to the meeting?" Mrs. Knox asked Mary-Larkin.

"I guess so," Mary-Larkin said.

The Knoxes looked disapprovingly at Mary-Larkin, and went on into the living room.

The Davenports came, and Mrs. Paget, Noble's mother.

"Are the Cobbs coming?" Mary-Larkin asked her mother.

"No, they flatly refused," Mrs. Thornhill said. "So did the Hubbards—Callie's parents."

A few more parents arrived, and then the Baptist minister, the Reverend Mr. Elton.

Mary-Larkin's mother scurried around seeing that everybody had coffee and cream and sugar and cookies. All this took quite a while. Why grownups took so long to drink a cup of coffee and eat a cookie was something Mary-Larkin had never understood.

Finally, Mr. Thornhill cleared his throat, and said, "Well, I guess we'd better begin. We asked you to come here to talk about Wheatley school. Our children have been assigned to Wheatley by court order, and we thought it might be a good idea to talk about some of the problems we might face and how we can deal with them. We have two young teachers from Wheatley with us tonight and I'm going to ask them to tell us a little bit about the school."

He nodded toward Miss Reeves.

"Well, it's a new building, you know," Miss Reeves

said. "It was named for Phyllis Wheatley, who was a black woman in Boston at the time of the Revolution. She was a poet. Last year, as we said, discipline was terrible. But we had a principal who didn't care. Students roamed the halls and never did any homework. But this year we'll have a new principal and some new students, and we think everything will be better.

"I don't think any of you need to be *afraid* to send your children to Wheatley. Even with the lack of discipline at Wheatley last year, we *loved* the *students*. They were great."

The Knoxes stared at her stonily. Mrs. Kingsley looked interested. Mrs. Paget looked blank.

"These young teachers seem so *dedicated*," Mrs. Kingsley said. "I think it's all going to *work*."

Mr. Kingsley nodded. Mrs. Thornhill said she thought Mrs. Kingsley was right.

"I can tell it's going to be a great year," Miss Reeves said.

"I don't," Mr. Knox spoke firmly and loudly. "It's not going to work. The court ruling says the Wheatley enrollment, with the district lines drawn the way they are, will be 65 percent black and 35 percent white. But already, we know that white families are moving out of the district that's been zoned into Wheatley. The Cobbs have bought a house, and other people are looking. I can assure you of that. It's going to be less than 35 percent white, and is that going to be safe? Be realistic," he said, looking at Miss Reeves. "Is it safe for a white child in a black school? It's all right for you, Mrs. Kingsley. You have a son." He paused, and looked at Mary-Larkin.

21

"But I don't want my daughter raped by a black boy!"

"None of us want our daughters raped, Mr. Knox," Mr. Thornhill said. "Not by black men, or white men, either. And I think we're all going to have to learn to not say 'boy' any more. But the schools of Stonewall will surely be safe for all people. Stonewall has a fair record on race relations . . . the lunch counters are open." He stopped and everybody remembered that Mr. Thornhill had helped to integrate the lunch counters. And everybody remembered that the swimming pool was still closed.

"I'm in the real estate business," Mr. Knox said, "and I say the Avondale section is doomed. White families are going to move out. You can't have a good neighborhood without good schools."

"But Avondale is the nicest part of town!" Mrs. Thornhill said. "The old houses. It's close to downtown."

"That won't matter, Mrs. Thornhill," said Mr. Knox. "Good white families aren't going to live here any more if they have to send their children to a black junior high and senior high. People with families won't buy here."

"If enough families stand firm and send their children to integrated schools, then the schools won't be black schools," Mr. Thornhill said. "We can show them that we can have good integrated schools in the inner-city area— if you can say Stonewall has an inner-city."

"Pardon me, Preacher," said Mr. Knox. "I can see why you have to take that stand. You have to live in the manse. But I'll be willing to bet money that before the year is out you come before the Session of the church and ask that the deacons sell this manse and buy a new one in Magnolia Gardens. I'm realistic!"

"Never," said Mrs. Thornhill.

Mr. Thornhill stood up. Mary-Larkin watched him. He was very pale, and she could tell that he was very angry. But he was still quiet, as he stood for a second, holding the back of a Victorian side chair, clutching the carving on it until his fingers were whiter than the china cups. He spoke very softly.

The room was very quiet, and everybody heard him.

"No, Mr. Knox, you'll lose your bet. I don't care if my daughter is the only white child in the whole town of Stonewall that goes to Phyllis Wheatley school, that's where she's going."

Mary-Larkin slipped out of the room and ran upstairs to her own room, and wept.

Chapter 5

After a while, Mary-Larkin got off her bed and wiped her eyes and blew her nose. She went in the bathroom and washed her face and then went into her brothers' room.

Joe was reading a book, and Luke was making a plastic airplane model.

"Did you hear what Papa just said?" she asked them.

Luke looked up guiltily. "Am I doing something wrong?" he asked.

"No, silly, what I mean is there's a meeting going on downstairs—"

"There's *always* a meeting going on downstairs," Joe interrupted.

"There's a meeting and everybody's parents are talking about Wheatley school and Papa just stood up and said I was going to Wheatley if I was the only white child in town that went to a black school!"

"When you get your school supplies, you better get a switchblade knife," Joe said.

"Oh, for heaven's sake! Don't you realize *you* have to go to Crispus Attucks? And you may be the only white kids there?"

"Yas, suh, boss," Joe said.

"Smart ass," said Mary-Larkin.

"What is to be will be," said Joe. "Don't you ever listen to Papa's sermons? It was all predestined before we were born."

"That's not what predestination is, and you know it," Mary-Larkin said.

Joe stared at her through his glasses. Like an owl, Mary-Larkin thought, but why weren't they more upset?

Luke spoke, as though he were answering Mary-Larkin's unspoken question.

"School is so bad anyway," he said. "What difference does it make?"

Mary-Larkin gave up. It was true, what Luke said, as far as the boys were concerned. Joe always made all A's and always got Excellent in conduct, and was so quiet and polite to everyone that he was a natural teacher-pleaser. It probably didn't make any difference to him which school he went to. And Luke was just the opposite —writing on the desk, never listening to the teacher, off in his fantasy world, wishing he were anywhere but in school; and so it didn't matter to him either whether he went to a white school or a black school or a purple school.

Mary-Larkin stalked out. Standing in the upstairs hall, she could hear the voices downstairs.

She recognized Mr. Elton, the Baptist preacher. "I often say that if God had intended the races to mix, he would have. . . ."

Mary-Larkin strained to hear the rest. She had heard the first part of the sentence many times, but she had never heard what it was that God would have done if he

25

had intended the races to mix. There was a clatter of cups, though, and Mary-Larkin missed the end again.

Mr. Elton was going on. "You'll notice that different species don't breed together; a robin doesn't mate with a crow."

Good grief, thought Mary-Larkin. He *is* stupid. Just the same, she told herself, I don't want to be a martyr. Why do I have to be the Joan of Arc to integrate Phyllis Wheatley Junior High School?

The next morning, she asked her mother the same question: "Why do I have to be the only one in town to integrate Phyllis Wheatley Junior High School?"

"Oh, you probably won't be the only one," Mrs. Thornhill said. "But you know what Kierkegaard says: 'The more people who believe something, the more apt it is to be wrong. The person who's right often has to stand alone.' "

"And you won't be alone," said Mr. Thornhill, coming into the kitchen.

"I know what you're going to say," Mary-Larkin said, "that I'll have the Holy Spirit with me. I'd rather have Missy Cobb any day than the Holy Spirit!"

"As a matter of fact, I wasn't thinking of the Holy Spirit," said Mr. Thornhill. "But I'm glad to see that you're aware of his presence. I was thinking of Crichton Kingsley. The Kingsleys are committed to sending Crichton to Wheatley. And Mrs. Paget is pretty sure she'll send Noble."

Noble. That would be neat, thought Mary-Larkin.

Chapter 6

On the first day of school, Mary-Larkin woke up early and lay in her bed looking out of the wavy windowpanes at the magnolia tree outside her window.

The burrs on the tree were getting red berries on them, a sure sign that summer was over, even though the weather was still hot.

School always started in Stonewall when it was still hot. Today was the day after Labor Day. Mary-Larkin understood from the books she had read that in most places school started in cool weather and girls wore skirts and sweaters on the first day. Not in Stonewall.

She squirmed in her bed and looked at the blue sky around the edges of the top of the magnolia. Once school had not been held in Stonewall because it snowed. It was the year Mary-Larkin was five, and she missed two days of kindergarten because of the snow.

Maybe it would snow today and she would not have to go to Phyllis Wheatley. Maybe it was all a bad dream—integration. But it wasn't. What could keep the schools from opening today? A hurricane? A race riot? *A race riot!* She didn't want a race riot.

She lay there and mourned. School was starting and she was going to the seventh grade at Phyllis Wheatley, not Longstreet. She would not be in the room with Missy or Callie Hubbard or Sarah Knox or Bruce Davenport—or anybody she knew, probably.

I prayed all summer that I wouldn't have to go to Wheatley, she thought. Was God dead?

Tears began to roll down Mary-Larkin's cheeks. To cry on the first day of school—that was awful! Mary-Larkin cried all the harder because she felt so bad that she had cried on the first day of school. The first day of school was a day to wear a new dress and carry new school supplies and have butterflies in your stomach and be excited. But not to cry!

"Mary-Larkin!"

Her mother was calling her.

"Mary-Larkin! Are you up?"

Her mother was coming upstairs. Mary-Larkin wiped her eyes on the sheet and rolled over on her side so she had her back to the door.

"Mary-Larkin! It's the first day of school!" Her mother knocked and came in. "Mary-Larkin!"

Mary-Larkin turned to face her mother.

"What's the matter, Mary-Larkin?"

"I don't want to go to school."

"Now, Mary-Larkin, you've just got the first-day-of-school jitters. It will be all right. Come on. I've got a coffee cake for breakfast. Come on. The boys are already up."

Mary-Larkin pulled the sheet over her head.

"Come on, Mary-Larkin. Come on. You *have* to go to school, so come on."

28

"Oh, all right," Mary-Larkin said from under the sheet.

"Come on, Baby Doll, come on." Mrs. Thornhill's voice quavered. She sounded upset.

Mary-Larkin peeked out from under the sheet and saw that her mother was upset. "Go on, Mama," she said. "I'll get up. I'll go."

Mrs. Thornhill turned and went out, and Mary-Larkin got up.

She stood by her wardrobe, peering in at her clothes, for a long time, and tried to decide what to wear. She finally put on a dress with a high waist that one of her aunts had sent her.

She slid into her sandals and went downstairs. I'm scared, she said to herself, I'm really scared.

She went to the kitchen and poured herself a glass of orange juice and a glass of milk and cut off a piece of coffee cake and took it all into the dining room. She had to make two trips.

"I thought coffee cake was for *happy* days," she said.

"It *is* a happy day," her father said, smiling. "This is the day the Lord has made. Rejoice and be glad in it."

"I knew you'd say that," Mary-Larkin said.

"Mary-Larkin, it is a happy day, because you're doing what's right." He looked at her. "Sometimes it's not easy to do what's right. Remember Abraham and Isaac. God told Abraham to sacrifice his son, the son that was born in his old age, and Abraham was ready to do it. You simply do what God tells you to, and its turns out all right."

"I didn't hear God tell me to go to Wheatley," Mary-Larkin said.

"Mary-Larkin, it will be all right," her father said, still smiling.

That was one good thing about Papa, Mary-Larkin thought. You could say outrageous things and he didn't get mad.

"I'm scared," she said out loud.

"What are you scared of?" he asked. "Let's analyze it. Are you scared because it's the first day of school? Are you scared because you're going to junior high school? Or are you scared because you're going to a school that's mostly black?"

"All three," said Mary-Larkin.

"That's perfectly natural," he said. "You wouldn't be alive and human if you weren't scared. But remember, there's no need to be afraid for your physical safety. This is America. Integration is the law of the land. This is 1970. The worst is over. And we've never had much trouble in Stonewall. We integrated the lunch counters without bloodshed. The swimming pool's not open yet, but that will probably work itself out next year. We wouldn't let you go to Wheatley if there was any danger of your being harmed in any way, Mary-Larkin. You know that."

"Yes, sir," Mary-Larkin said. She felt better. Papa was crazy, all right, but he wasn't as crazy as she thought he was some of the time. Of course, he wouldn't let her go to Wheatley if there was anything to be afraid of.

She munched on her coffee cake. Joe and Luke came in and got their breakfast. Mrs. Thornhill came in and sat down at the table and had a cup of coffee. When they were all finished, Mr. Thornhill read from the Bible, Psalm 112:

"Happy is the man who fears the Lord
   and finds great joy in his commandments . . .
Bad news shall have no terrors for him,
   because his heart is steadfast, trusting in the Lord."

"Let's pray," he said, and the Thornhills bowed their heads.

"We're the only family in Stonewall that still has family prayers," Mary-Larkin said when it was over.

"No, we're not," Mrs. Thornhill said. "I know the Pettys still have family prayers." Dr. Petty was the old, white-haired retired preacher, the pastor-emeritus of the First Presbyterian Church.

Mary-Larkin had to laugh—of course, the Pettys had family prayers. "But they don't have any children," she said.

"It isn't how many people do a thing that makes it right," Mr. Thornhill said.

"I knew you were going to say that," Mary-Larkin said.

"Get your things, Mary-Larkin, and I'll take you to school," Mrs. Thornhill said.

Mary-Larkin was astonished. She had always had to walk to school before. She ran up the stairs and got her purse and her new ring binder, which was full of new notebook paper.

"Have you got lunch money?" Mrs. Thornhill asked.

"No, ma'am."

"If I can find my purse. . . ."

"Have you got your car keys?" Mary-Larkin asked.

Together they found Mrs. Thornhill's purse and car keys and Mrs. Thornhill gave Mary-Larkin three dollar bills for lunch money for the week. "Now that you're in

31

junior high, you can handle a week's money at one time," she told her. Mary-Larkin felt very grown-up.

Mrs. Thornhill kissed Joe and Luke good-bye.

"Have a nice day at Crispus Attucks," she said. "Papa will walk down with you today."

Joe and Luke looked at her skeptically.

Mrs. Thornhill and Mary-Larkin went out to the car.

"I'm going to pick up Critter," Mrs. Thornhill said. "I'll take you all in the morning and Mrs. Kingsley will bring you all home."

"I always wanted to be in a car pool," Mary-Larkin said.

"We thought it might be nicer right at first. . . ." Mrs. Thornhill murmured.

They drove to the Kingsley's house and Critter was standing on the sidewalk, holding a new ring binder with pictures of spacecraft on it. His shirttail was already half out of his jeans. He got in the car and replied politely to Mrs. Thornhill's greeting. Then he looked out the car window.

"Are you scared?" Mary-Larkin asked him.

"No," he said, and kept looking out the window.

They drove down Riggs Street and across Broad and up to Phyllis Wheatley school. It was a new building of gray concrete and it looked a little like a fort.

"Where do we go?" Mary-Larkin said. "What do we do?"

"I'll go in with you," Mrs. Thornhill said. "You're both preregistered. We'll find out where seventh graders go."

They got out of the car and walked through an iron gate and into a courtyard, the center of the Wheatley building. The yard had small trees in it and big planter boxes. The building that wrapped around it was three stories tall with open galleries on all three floors. She liked the building once she was in the courtyard. She kept staring up at the galleries to avoid looking at the students who almost filled the yard. Her first fleeting impression, when they walked in, was that everybody else was black. When she lowered her eyes and looked again, she still felt that everyone else was black. She saw no white people. Students sat on the planters, leaned against trees and gallery columns, or sat on the courtyard pavement. Everyone seemed quiet since they had walked in.

The students were staring at them.

Mary-Larkin felt sick. She was scared. She decided she must be coming down with flu—she felt that bad.

"Why, hello, Mary-Larkin, how are you? You're in my homeroom." It was Miss Reeves, one of the teachers who had come to the meeting at her house. Mary-Larkin had never been so glad to see anyone in her life.

Miss Reeves looked at Critter. "Are you a seventh grader, too?"

Mrs. Thornhill introduced Critter.

"Crichton Kingsley," said Miss Reeves. "You're in my homeroom, too. I'll take you up."

Mrs. Thornhill kissed Mary-Larkin's cheek. "Goodbye, Baby Doll," she said.

"That girl is named Baby Doll," said one of the young men students. He said it very loudly, and there was a ripple of laughter in the courtyard.

Mary-Larkin tried to tell herself that it was just the kind of thing any boy—white or black—would say, and followed Miss Reeves up to her third-floor room.

Chapter 7

"You're in my first-period English class, too," Miss Reeves said. "Right after homeroom. But we probably won't have classes today. I think it's going to take a while to get organized."

When the bell rang for school to start, there were only a handful of students in Miss Reeves' room. More straggled in.

Seventh graders, it turned out, were supposed to stop by the auditorium and get their homerooms.

Annette Deshay came in the room about nine o'clock. Mary-Larkin remembered her from Millie Bybee school, but she hadn't known her well. As the day wore on, it turned out that Annette and Critter and Mary-Larkin were the only white students in Miss Reeves' homeroom. There were nineteen black students.

The public address system kept popping on and different voices made announcements.

"Opening day is bound to be confusing," Miss Reeves explained, "with all this zoning and new districts and all."

Miss Reeves tried to make everybody welcome and had the students introduce themselves to each other. After a while, she got out a book and began to read out loud to them. She read a story, *The Red Pony*, and then she began to read poetry, poems like "Casey at the Bat" and one by Woody Guthrie.

The public address system kept telling them to stay in their homerooms, until certain problems were ironed out.

Annette Deshay came and sat by Mary-Larkin and said, "I'm scared."

Mary-Larkin had built up a little more confidence by that time, and she said, "It's all right." But she didn't really have her heart in it.

Annette Deshay had lanky hair and she wore knee socks, and Mary-Larkin felt a little sorry for her.

At first, the black students ignored the three white students. But then, in the middle of the morning, the black girls began to glance at Annette and Mary-Larkin, and one or two smiled at them. The black young men seemed determined to pretend they didn't exist.

Critter stared out of the window.

Would Critter be in trouble all the time in junior high the way he'd been in Millie Bybee? Mary-Larkin wondered. The teachers had always yelled at Critter and told him he wasn't living up to his potential. He was always being sent to the principal's office. One time, he had had to sit at a desk all by himself in the back corner of the classroom for a whole week. He had used the time, she recalled, to write an epic poem about a knight called Sir Kriton. He had written it on pages and pages of lined notebook paper, and the teacher had looked at it one day and said, "This is very creative, Crichton, but you must learn to punctuate properly."

Miss Reeves was summoned to the office by the public address system. She came back with their registration forms and they all began to fill them out. Mary-Larkin was working on hers when the black girl in front of her turned around and looked at her form. Then she showed Mary-Larkin *her* form.

Mary-Larkin looked at her name, Vanella Brasher, and then saw that they had exactly the same birthday— May 28, 1958.

Vanella was especially nice to Mary-Larkin after that, and Mary-Larkin began to feel better.

Vanella was an attractive girl with a wide smile. Her skin was the color of maple syrup; her hair was straightened, and she wore a skirt and cotton knit top that Mary-Larkin liked.

(She knew her parents always said it was wrong to judge people by their clothes—whether they wore knee socks or not, or whether they had on nice-looking tops— and she reminded herself not to mention anybody's clothes when she got home.)

If I ever get home, she thought.

She watched Vanella talking to the other black girls— they all seemed to know each other. Except for one especially quiet girl named Jimmi-Jo, who sat in the back of the room and never said anything.

Mary-Larkin noticed that the black girls talked about their hair as much as white girls did—they had all spent a lot of time and effort straightening their hair for school, she gathered.

The day stretched endlessly. At last Miss Reeves got word on the intercom that she could take her homeroom to lunch.

They all filed out and started down the gallery to the stairway. Mary-Larkin had already decided that she disliked the stairways. She liked the galleries that served as corridors, but she hated the enclosed stairways that were dark and noisy with heavy doors at the top and the bottom.

Annette Deshay walked beside her as they went down the stairs, but a young man came and pushed her aside. "Baby Doll, lend me some lunch money."

Mary-Larkin looked at him, as they went down the stairs. He was very tall and black. She was scared again. She didn't know what to say. The young man kept in step with her and kept looking at her.

"Come on, Baby Doll," he said.

Slowly, Mary-Larkin opened her purse and took out her change purse. She saw the three dollar bills there. "I don't have any change," she said.

"A dollar is okay," he said.

He grabbed one of the dollars and shot down the rest of the stairs. Mary-Larkin nervously closed her purse and stumbled down the rest of the steps.

Annette caught up with her. "What is that boy's name?" Mary-Larkin asked her.

"Which one?" Annette said. "I can't tell them apart."

"Ssssh," said Mary-Larkin. "Don't let them hear you say things like that."

"I don't care," Annette said.

They followed the crowd toward the lunchroom, which

37

was down at one end of the courtyard, and as they were standing in line for food service, another boy came up to Mary-Larkin and said, "Can I borrow a dollar?"

Mary-Larkin stared at him.

"Can I have a dollar?" he said again.

"No," Mary-Larkin said. She didn't know the boy and couldn't decide whether he was in her homeroom or not. Annette was right, even though you couldn't say things like that out loud.

"It's my lunch money for the whole week," she said to him.

"I'll pay you back," he said.

"Oh, all right," Mary-Larkin said. She gave him a dollar, and immediately, another boy came up and asked her for a dollar.

"I can't," she said, "I have to buy my lunch. I can't."

"Your lunch won't cost but fifty cents," he said.

A grain of determination was growing into a pebble inside of Mary-Larkin. "Wait until I get my lunch," she said, "and I'll see."

The boy left and joined a crowd at a table. They all laughed loudly at something he said. Mary-Larkin felt sick again and looked away. She told herself that all boys tried to show off and bluster around girls, not just black boys.

"Here comes another one," Annette said. Mary-Larkin watched an approaching boy.

This one went to Annette, though.

"Let me have some dust," he said.

"What?" Annette said.

"Dust," he said. "I need lunch money."

Mary-Larkin looked ahead to see what there was for

lunch, but she wheeled back when Annette screamed.

"He stuck his hand up my dress!" Annette screeched. "Mary-Larkin, that boy stuck his hand up my dress! AEEEEEEEeeeeeee!"

Everybody in the lunchroom was staring at them. Annette, still screaming, ran out of the lunchroom.

Mary-Larkin stayed in line and got a plate lunch. Where had Annette gone? Had someone indeed stuck his hand up her dress? How horrible. What if somebody stuck his hand up *my* dress? she thought. Papa had said there wasn't any physical danger. But there was, wasn't there?

She paid for her lunch, and stood with her tray by the cashier, uncertain about what to do.

"Over here, Mary-Larkin!"

She looked toward the voice. It was Vanella. She was sitting at the table with some other black girls and Mary-Larkin thankfully made her way toward them.

She thought all the girls at the table were in her home-room, but she wasn't sure, so she tried to eat and smile a lot at the same time. The result was she dropped a lot of spaghetti on her dress. Oh, well.

The girls really didn't look alike at all the way they had seemed to at first, Mary-Larkin decided, but just the same it was going to be hard to learn all their names. Vanella, of course, was Vanella, pretty and lively. Augusta was the tall funny one with the deep voice. The quiet one, Jimmi-Jo, was new to the neighborhood. Like Missy, she wore clothes that met Mary-Larkin's standards.

While Mary-Larkin was eating her chocolate pudding, a boy came up and borrowed her last fifty cents.

"You shouldn't have done that," Vanella said.

"Won't he pay me back?" Mary-Larkin asked.

The girls all laughed. "Won't Major pay her back?" they asked each other and laughed.

"What's his name?" Mary-Larkin asked.

"Major Mills," Vanella said.

Mary-Larkin looked around the lunchroom, looking for the boys who had borrowed the two other dollars. But she couldn't be sure which ones they were. Surely that boy in the football jersey was one of them . . . or was it that other boy over there in another jersey?

Looking around, she noticed a sprinkling of white students in the lunchroom, but nobody she knew very well. There was Critter, at the table with Major Mills. Where was Noble Paget? she wondered. After lunch they went back to Miss Reeves' room, and Miss Reeves said they were going to run a short schedule that afternoon. She had their schedule cards. They would go to each of their classes for twenty minutes, she said.

Annette did not appear before they left homeroom. After twenty minutes of English, Mary-Larkin went to French, then to history, then to math, then to art, then physical education.

Critter was in nearly all her classes, but he always sat by a window and looked out. Mary-Larkin sat by Vanella every chance she got.

Vanella Brasher had become a refuge for her, a friendly face in a strange world.

Chapter 8

After school, Mary-Larkin trudged through the courtyard to the street to look for Mrs. Kingsley.

She saw that, unlike white schools, Wheatley had no
line of parents in automobiles waiting to pick up children. There was only one car parked in front, and it was
Mrs. Kingsley's.

Mary-Larkin got in.

"Hello, Mary-Larkin, how was the first day of
school?" Mrs. Kingsley asked.

"Awful," Mary-Larkin said.

Critter appeared and got in and his mother asked him
how the first day had been and he said, merely, "Okay,"
and looked out the window. Mary-Larkin realized that
Critter had spent the entire day looking out windows.

Mrs. Kingsley let Mary-Larkin out in front of the
manse, and she walked up the brick walk, scuffing
magnolia leaves and kicking at the burrs that had fallen
off the trees. Mrs. Thornhill must have been watching for
her because she opened the front door before Mary-
Larkin put her foot on the bottom step.

She reached out to hug Mary-Larkin, but Mary-Larkin walked steadily past her.

"How was it?" Mrs. Thornhill asked.

"Ghastly!" Mary-Larkin said, and threw her notebook down on the hall table and kept going to the kitchen. Mrs. Thornhill followed her.

"Mama, it *was* awful!" Mary-Larkin said. "There wasn't anybody there I knew! Not a soul!"

"Critter was there. . . ."

"I mean anybody I *really* know. None of my friends were there. Not Callie or Sarah or Noble Paget or anybody."

"Where was everybody?"

"I don't know, Mama, but they weren't at Phyllis Wheatley."

"You mean there weren't any other white students but you and Critter?"

"There were a few, but nobody I knew. Annette Deshay—you know, that went to Millie Bybee—she was there, but she disappeared at lunch time after a black boy stuck his hand up her dress."

"My gracious! What?"

Mary-Larkin told her mother about the incident in the lunchroom, and added, "I lost my lunch money."

"Lost your lunch money?"

"For the whole week."

"What happened?"

"Boys borrowed it."

"Won't they pay it back?"

"Vanella said they wouldn't. She said they always tried to get money from people."

"Who is Vanella?"

"She's a nice girl. Black. Our birthdays are the same. She was nice to me. But it's awful, Mama. We didn't do anything all morning—just sat around." Mary-Larkin began to cry. "Mama, I can't go back."

"Yes, you can," Mrs. Thornhill said, but her voice was not as firm as it usually was.

"I CAN'T GO BACK! I CAN'T!" Mary-Larkin said.

"Hush. Don't get hysterical. There were bound to be some shocks, I guess."

"I knew you wouldn't care," Mary-Larkin said.

"Of course, I care. Don't be silly. But right is right."

"All you care about is if a thing is right or wrong. What if I'm miserable?"

"You won't be miserable for long," Mrs. Thornhill said. "Look, I made some Tollhouse cookies."

Mary-Larkin was still crying. Mrs. Thornhill made ice-box cookies by the gross, but Tollhouse cookies were a real treat, usually reserved for birthdays or other special occasions.

"I'd choke on them," Mary-Larkin said. "Carbohydrates don't solve everything."

She went upstairs to her room. She cried some more and then got up and washed her face and called Missy Cobb.

Missy said the first day at Longstreet had been really cool. She was in the homeroom with Callie Hubbard and they had both signed up for mixed chorus.

"How did Callie get to go to Longstreet?" Mary-Larkin asked. "She was in the Wheatley district."

"She gave a phony address," Missy said. "Lot of kids did. Monk Stevens and Denise did, I know."

Mary-Larkin felt outrage at a trick like that and then

43

regret that her own parents were so terribly honest.

"Are you going tomorrow?" Missy asked her.

"Where?"

"The Gadabouts' party."

"I forgot about it," Mary-Larkin said. "I don't even know. I guess so. I'll have to ask Mama."

The Gadabout Club was the social club for junior high school girls in Stonewall. Every year the Gadabouts had a Coke party the day after school started to which all the "nice" girls were invited. They had a dance during the Christmas holidays, too. Members of the Assembly, the social group for senior high school girls, were selected from the Gadabouts.

"My parents may not let me go," Mary-Larkin said. "The Gadabouts *exclude* people."

"Oh, no," Missy said, horrified.

"I'm just kidding," Mary-Larkin said. "Even *my* parents can't be that crazy."

Mary-Larkin went downstairs and found that Joe and Luke were home and they said, between bites of Toll-house cookies, that Crispus Attucks was "okay," and "as good as any school could be."

Luke even volunteered a piece of information.

"My teacher played the radio during school," he said. He looked *happy*.

Little brothers were creeps, Mary-Larkin thought. No, they were *insensitive*. She said it out loud, and liked the sound of it.

Mary-Larkin's father came home and asked her about Phyllis Wheatley. She told him everything.

"It's a form of testing," he said about the lunch

money. "Don't worry about it. Just take one day's lunch money at a time, and then you won't have any extra to lend. The business with Annette is just another form of testing, too. You see you all are strangers in the school—and the young people are reacting. Things are bound to get better. You'll look back on this first day and laugh." But Mr. Thornhill was genuinely shocked at how few white students had turned up at Phyllis Wheatley. "I had no idea it would be this bad," he said. "White flight! If everybody would stick together on this, there would be enough white students in the black schools to have a good racial mix. Oh, well, the situation may stabilize."

Mary-Larkin then asked if she could go to the Gadabouts' party.

"The Gadabouts is such a silly club," Mrs. Thornhill said.

"Please, Mama. I want to see my friends," Mary-Larkin said. Her voice trembled.

"I guess it's all right," Mrs. Thornhill said doubtfully.

"I want to see some white people some of the time," she said.

"You'll see white people at church," her father said. "It's ironic that the schools are integrated, but our church is not."

He looked sad and discouraged. Mary-Larkin wondered how to cheer him up. She could say that Wheatley wasn't all that bad, but it would be a lie.

She went back upstairs to call Missy.

45

Chapter 9

Mary-Larkin got ready for school the next day feeling desperate. She *knew* Wheatley was bad today; yesterday she had only *feared* it would be bad.

She wore her navy-blue sailor dress, though, because of the Gadabouts' party.

When they got to school that morning, Critter wandered off across the courtyard and Mary-Larkin stood by the gate and looked around.

The girls at Wheatley seemed to wear anything they wanted to to school. There must not be a dress code the way there was at Longstreet, she thought, because the girls wore dresses, minis, maxis, pantsuits, jeans, and even hot pants.

She looked around for Annette Deshay and didn't see her.

"Mary-Larkin!"

She turned, and saw Vanella. Gratefully, she walked over to Vanella and stood with her and her friends until the bell rang for homeroom.

Several boys asked her for money, but Mary-Larkin

told them, quite truthfully, that she had only enough money for her own lunch that day. She heard one boy mutter something about "honky bitch" as she turned away, but she shrugged it off.

"You ought to just bring your lunch like we do," Vanella said.

"I guess I will," Mary-Larkin said.

The day passed uneventfully—Mary-Larkin did not see Annette Deshay—and after school, Mrs. Kingsley was waiting and said she'd drop Mary-Larkin off at the Gadabouts' party.

Critter got in and they drove off. When they got to the Dabneys' big house in Magnolia Gardens, the yard was full of junior high school girls.

Critter put his hands over his ears. "I can't stand that giggling," he said. "You can hear it blocks away."

When the girls saw Mary-Larkin getting out of the car, they all turned and ran toward her, squealing.

"Mary-Larkin!"

"How was it!"

"We miss you!"

They enveloped her, those girls, and Mary-Larkin reveled in the warm bath of attention.

"What is it like at Wheatley?" someone asked, as all her old friends stood in a circle around her.

"It's terrible," Mary-Larkin said. "It's terrible."

"Oooooh." The sound rose from the cluster of girls.

"There's not one girl I know there," Mary-Larkin said. "Annette Deshay was there yesterday but she didn't come back today."

"She was at Longstreet today!" Callie Hubbard said.

"She went to the doctor and he gave her a certificate saying it would do her psychological damage to go to Wheatley. She said a boy tried to rape her."

"Good grief," Mary-Larkin said. "It wasn't that bad. What really happened was a boy stuck his hand up her dress—or she said he did—while we were standing in the lunchroom. She ran out of the lunchroom screaming."

"I don't blame her," Sarah Knox said. "My father says you're going to get raped at Wheatley."

Mary-Larkin loathed Wheatley and wanted more than anything else in the world to be at Longstreet, but even so, she couldn't believe she'd be raped at Wheatley. "I'll be deviled to death about money, but that's the worst part," she said, and told them about what had happened the first day.

"That's awful," Missy said.

"Tell me everything about Longstreet," Mary-Larkin said. "Tell me about everybody."

"Well, Sarah Knox and Mell Stockton and Deborah Long and Clyde Patterson are all at private school," Callie said.

"The Christian Academy in the Baptist church?" Mary-Larkin said.

"That's right," Callie said.

"How do you like it, Sarah?" she asked.

"It's okay," Sarah said.

"How did you give a false address, Callie?" Mary-Larkin asked her. "Did you make one up?"

"Oh, I'm supposed to be living with my aunt," Callie said. "We gave her address. She lives in the Longstreet district."

"Denise and Monk Stevens did that, too," Missy said.

"What about Noble Paget?" Mary-Larkin asked.

"Where's he?"

"He's at Longstreet," Callie said.

"How?"

"I don't know," Missy said. "He didn't move."

"Poor Mary-Larkin! Can't you do *anything?*" said Sarah. "Are your folks going to make you stay at Wheatley all year?"

"I'm sure they will," Mary-Larkin said.

"And there's nobody from Millie Bybee there?"

"Well, there's Critter Kingsley."

"Critter!" The scorn in Missy's voice dismissed him.

"Is he still as crazy as ever?" Callie said.

The girls drank Cokes and ate chips and dips and chattered about life at Longstreet and the Christian Academy. Mary-Larkin drank it up.

Seventh graders at Longstreet had their own football teams and their own cheerleaders.

Missy and Denise and Callie were all signed up to try out for seventh-grade cheerleaders.

"I don't even know if Wheatley has seventh-grade cheerleaders," Mary-Larkin said. "If they do, I'll try out, too."

"You ought to," Missy said. "You were getting good this summer."

"Are you going to try out, Sarah?" someone asked.

"We don't even have football teams, yet," Sarah moaned. "They say we will, though."

"That's too bad," Mary-Larkin said.

"It's not as bad as going to a black school," Sarah snapped.

Chapter 10

The next day, the third day of life at Wheatley, Mary-Larkin went to school carrying her lunch in a paper bag and wearing a rather grim air of resignation.

Right after homeroom, there was an assembly of the student body in the auditorium.

The principal came out on the stage and talked to them. His name was Mr. Searle, and he was tall, and he was very black. He was certainly different from Miss Blessing, the principal at Millie Bybee, and different, too, from the principal at Longstreet, who had come to Millie Bybee to tell the sixth graders about life in junior high.

While she listened to the announcements Mr. Searle made, she was looking at him and trying to figure out what it was that made him so impressive. He had a strong personality, she decided. You had to watch him when he talked. He demanded attention even when he just stood there. The students got really quiet for the first time since Mary-Larkin had been at Wheatley school.

He wore exotic clothes—a maroon suit and maroon

shirt and a white tie—and he reminded Mary-Larkin of some of the tropical birds she'd seen in the Atlanta zoo.

"We want you to learn how to behave in the world today while you are here," Mr. Searle was saying.

"We are here to help each other. And we are going to help each other by having order at Wheatley school. We're going to have order so we can learn and so we can help each other. We can't open your heads and pour it in, but we can put it here before you and we can arrange the situation so you can put it in yourself.

"We don't have many rules at Wheatley, but we're going to have a new rule here for a while. That rule is that everybody in this school is going to call everybody by his right name. This is to expound each person with dignity."

Mary-Larkin was impressed, in spite of that odd use of the word, expound. He made it sound important, all right.

Several teachers were on the stage to make announcements. Miss Horn, the pretty, black, physical education teacher, announced that seventh-grade cheerleader tryouts would begin that afternoon after school.

Mary-Larkin, of course, wanted to stay for that. After school she went outside to tell Mrs. Kingsley she wouldn't be going home.

"And Critter's staying for football practice," Mrs. Kingsley said. "I'll just come back when you all call me up."

She was very nice about it, Mary-Larkin thought.

The would-be cheerleaders for the seventh grade gathered around Miss Horn, who stood on the lawn behind the school. She was writing the girls' names down on a clipboard.

"This is the way we'll do it, girls," Miss Horn said when she had everybody's name. "We'll let each one of you demonstrate one cheer. I'll choose the best ten of you to try out for the seventh-grade assembly and the students will choose five of those."

Vanella was there with Lanett and Wynona from Mary-Larkin's homeroom. Miss Horn called on Vanella first, and Vanella was very good. She was graceful and well coordinated and she had practiced—you could tell that.

She led a cheer Mary-Larkin had never heard before, "S–O–U–L, S–O–U–L!"

Lots of the girls were good, Mary-Larkin noted. And the black girls all used cheers she'd never heard before. She began to be afraid that there were more than ten who were better than she was. But when Miss Horn called her name, she trotted over in front of the group and announced, "I'll do 'Hit 'em a lick.' "

"All right," said Miss Horn.

Mary-Larkin went through the motions, just as she and Missy had practiced all summer . . . kneeling, standing, rolling motion with the arms, the leap at the end. She felt that she was okay, and that was all.

She sat down by Vanella for the rest of the tryouts.

"You all are real good," Miss Horn said when they were all through. "It's hard to choose. Let's see. I think we'll let twelve of you try out on stage—Vanella Brasher, Wynona Harris, Lanett Lewis, . . ." the names went on. And then Mary-Larkin heard her own name ". . . and Mary-Larkin Thornhill. All of you meet me here

52

tomorrow afternoon and we'll practice a little before you go before the assembly."

The winners were all being congratulated—except Mary-Larkin. But then Vanella came over and said, "You were good, Mary-Larkin."

"Thanks," Mary-Larkin said, "but I'm not as good as you all are."

Mary-Larkin picked up her books and started off. She had to call Mrs. Kingsley. Where was Critter? Was football practice over? She went in the courtyard, which was empty, and found the office door locked.

There was no pay phone at Wheatley that she knew of. She went back out to the lawn to find Miss Horn, but Miss Horn was gone.

She went out to the front of the school, and there was, of course, no sign of Mrs. Kingsley.

Wheatley straddled the line between a white neighborhood and a black neighborhood. Vanella and Lanett and the others had already left the school, headed in the opposite direction from the one Mary-Larkin must take.

Well, she'd just walk home, she decided. It wasn't all that far. She started off down Riggs Street.

She walked past an automobile repair garage, a grocery store, where two men lounged, and a dry-cleaning place.

When she stopped before crossing a busy street, she looked around and behind her at the mean and dingy neighborhood through which she had walked, and saw Critter walking down Riggs Street.

She stood there and waited for him, and Critter began to run to catch up with her.

"Hi!" he said, and he smiled at her.

Mary-Larkin had never seen Critter smile before. The smile was—Mary-Larkin could only think of the word "sweet," which wasn't what she wanted to say—but the smile made her suddenly feel shy with Critter. "Hi," she said.

They walked down Riggs together in silence. At Broad, they stopped for the traffic light.

"How was football practice?" Mary-Larkin finally asked him.

"All right, I guess," Critter said. "I'm the token honky, I guess. It seems to me they sure do tackle me hard—but then I've never played anything but Pee Wee football before."

"Do they tackle you hard because you're white?"

"I don't know," Critter said.

"My father says they're testing," Mary-Larkin said.

"I hope I pass," Critter said. "Hey, did you hear what happened? To Aubrey Little?"

"Who's Aubrey Little?"

"He's that little boy in the seventh grade, a white boy. He's not in any of my classes but physical education. But you must see him around."

"Is he that little-bitty guy with the tow hair?"

"That's the one," Critter said. "Well, he had an operation before school started. For hernia. So he doesn't suit up for P.E. Today at P.E., he was just standing around on the playground over by the fence, you know, just mooching around while everybody else ran laps. And three black guys jumped the fence and mugged him."

"Mugged him!"

"Well, not exactly mugged him. But they robbed him."

"How much money did he have?" Mary-Larkin asked.

"I don't think he had but twenty-five cents or so," Critter said. "But they took all he had."

"Poor Aubrey," Mary-Larkin said.

"But then there was some real excitement. In his next class, his teacher was Miss Bowling and she noticed him. Do you know Miss Bowling?"

"Yes, she came to our house for a meeting," Mary-Larkin said.

"Everybody goes to your house for meetings," Critter said. "Anyway, she noticed Aubrey looked kind of funny and she knew he'd had that operation, and so she asked him what was the matter. He told her what happened and she took him right down to the principal's office."

"To Mr. Searle?"

"Yeah, and Mr. Searle took Aubrey and the two of them went all around the neighborhood, into every beer joint around the school. And in one beer joint, Aubrey saw the three men and he pointed them out. And Mr. Searle called the police and the police came and arrested the three men and took them away. Aubrey was sure proud of himself when he came back to the school."

"That's great," Mary-Larkin said.

"Mr. Searle said he wanted the community to know that he wasn't going to have that kind of thing going on around Phyllis Wheatley school . . . and he told Aubrey to tell everybody what happened. So Aubrey stopped me and told me."

"That's pretty neat," Mary-Larkin said. "Little old pale Aubrey. And he got to go in all those beer joints." Mary-Larkin thought of those mysterious dark places in unpainted shacks with signs that said JOE'S BEER AND HOT SANDWICHES and MARY BELL'S GOOD EATS.

"And during school, too," Critter said. "See you," he said at her corner, and left her and began to run home.

Mary-Larkin walked home alone.

Chapter 11

That night at home, it was Joe and Luke who were the center of attention.

They came home late, and they had been in a fight. Joe had a black eye; Luke's lip was cut; they were both dirty and their shirts were torn.

"What happened?" Mr. Thornhill asked.

Joe tried to divert his father by telling in endless detail the story of a movie they had seen in school, and Luke mentioned the high price of chocolate milk in the school lunchroom, but Mr. Thornhill was not diverted.

"What happened?" he asked again.

"We got in a fight," Luke said.

"Look, Pop," said Joe, "we're not allowed to say 'nigger,' are we?"

"No," Mr. Thornhill said quietly. "Of course not."

"Well, we didn't," Luke said.

"Look, it's okay now, Pop," Joe said.

"It really is," Luke said. "They'll leave us alone now."

"We're kind of friends," Joe said.

"What happened?" Mr. Thornhill said.

"They called us 'honkies,' " Luke said.

"And we didn't call them 'niggers,' " Joe said. "We knew we couldn't, so we called them 'little black mother-fuckers.' "

Mr. Thornhill turned away, hiding a smile, but Mrs. Thornhill giggled.

Mary-Larkin laughed, too. All the Thornhills stood around the kitchen laughing as hard as they could. Mrs. Thornhill wiped tears from her eyes, Mr. Thornhill's face turned red from laughing, and Mary-Larkin's stomach hurt she laughed so much.

They all felt better after the laughing spree.

"Listen, just don't ever use words like that again," Mrs. Thornhill said.

"Especially around *my* friends," Mary-Larkin said.

"I advise you not to call your schoolmates names like that either," Mr. Thornhill said.

"We won't, Papa," Luke said. "We told you we got it all settled this afternoon. Really, we're *friends* now. It's okay."

At the supper table, Mary-Larkin told about the assembly and Mr. Searle's new rule. "See, he's trying to avoid you all calling each other 'honky' and 'nigger,' " Mrs. Thornhill said.

Then Mary-Larkin told them about Aubrey Little's adventure, and the grown-up Thornhills were more impressed with Mr. Searle.

"He sounds wonderful," Mr. Thornhill said. "He acted at once to show the community he wasn't going to have that kind of thing going on, and he acted at once to make Aubrey Little a hero instead of a victim. He must be a very good principal."

"I hadn't thought of it like that," Mary-Larkin said.

The next morning, Friday, Mary-Larkin lost her car pool. "You won't mind walking home, will you?" her mother said. "Critter has to stay for football practice and you'll be staying for things, too. Mrs. Kingsley and I have decided it's perfectly safe for you all to walk home in the afternoons. We will take turns driving you to school in the mornings, since it is a little farther away than Longstreet. How's that?"

"Terrible," said Mary-Larkin. "The only nice thing about going to Wheatley was the car pool. I should have known it was too good to be true."

"Well, I'll pick you up on days you have a piano lesson. I guess you'll start them next week."

"Oh, all right."

When they got to school, Critter slid away, and Mary-Larkin looked around the courtyard for Vanella and the other girls in her homeroom. She found them over by a pyracantha tree in a big planter box and walked over.

By now, she had sorted out several black faces and put names to them. She knew Vanella, of course, and Lanett. And Wynona. And Jimmi-Jo, who was very quiet. And Augusta. Augusta was tall and skinny and funny. She turned and looked down at Mary-Larkin now and said, "Where you stay?"

"What?" asked Mary-Larkin.

"Where you *stay*?" Augusta repeated.

"Stay?" Mary-Larkin repeated. And at last it dawned

59

on her. What Augusta meant was, where do you live?

"Oh, I stay down on the other side of Broad Street," she said. "On Church Street."

"Way down there?" Augusta said. "Where that boy stay? That white boy. What's his name?"

"Critter," Mary-Larkin said. "Critter lives close to me. On Battle Street." She hesitated. "His real name is Crichton."

"He your boyfriend?" Augusta asked.

"Good heavens, no," Mary-Larkin said. She was furious.

"He looks at you a lot," Augusta said.

"He's a real nut," Mary-Larkin said.

"Who is your boyfriend?" Lanett asked.

"I don't have a boyfriend," Mary-Larkin said. She thought, fleetingly, and painfully, of Noble Paget. She shifted her feet around, and tried to think of something light and funny to say. "I guess I'll be an old maid."

The girls laughed. "Oh, no baby, you'll get married," Vanella reassured her.

The bell rang and they all went into Miss Reeves' room. Mary-Larkin was still surprised at how few rules about clothes there were at Wheatley. Three boys in the room had on hats, and two wore dark glasses.

Although she was getting to know the girls, she was sure of the names of only two boys—Major Mills was tall and the class clown. Roosevelt Dobb was his best friend and straight man. While she was looking around the class at the faces, announcements came over the public address system as they did every morning. She wrote down the time and date of the seventh-grade assembly when the cheerleaders would be chosen.

60

There would be a meeting next week, too, the P.A. system said, to organize a P.T.A. at Wheatley. "Tell your parents," the mechanical voice said.

Miss Reeves was talking now, about free lunches. More than half the class got up to get free lunch cards from Miss Reeves. What was it? Had she missed something?

She turned around and asked Vanella what free lunch cards were.

"For *welfare*," Vanella hissed at her. "We have to show a card in the lunchroom to get a free lunch."

Mary-Larkin felt her face flame. These kids were on *welfare*. They were really poor, she realized. Even Vanella, cute, popular Vanella.

Miss Reeves was now dealing with excuses for absences the day before. Mary-Larkin sighed with boredom. She had looked forward to junior high and it had turned out to be like this, just plain boring.

Homeroom period was now over officially—the bell had rung—and it was time for English to begin.

"Since we don't have any books yet—" Miss Reeves began.

"Why don't we have books?" Mary-Larkin asked her.

"Mr. Searle likes for us to wait to make sure the students stay in the room and stay in the school," Miss Reeves said. "You know, the school is responsible for the textbooks if a student loses one or takes one and doesn't pay for it or bring it back. So in this school, we wait to give out textbooks for a while."

Another mark against Wheatley, Mary-Larkin thought. Missy and Callie had their books already at Longstreet, she knew.

"I can either read aloud to you," Miss Reeves said, "or we can do grammar drills."

"READ ALOUD," chorused the class.

Miss Reeves loved to read aloud.

Today she read poetry. It was different from any poetry she had ever read. It was from a book, *Understanding Black Poetry*, and Miss Reeves read a poem about God and some boys at a pool hall and both of these, she said, were by a black woman named Gwendolyn Brooks.

"Read that one again," Major Mills said with authority.

Miss Reeves read it again. It was called, " 'We Real Cool'—The Pool Players. Seven at the Golden Shovel."

> "We real cool.   We
> Left school.   We
>
> Lurk late.   We
> Strike straight.   We
>
> Sing sin.   We
> Thin gin.   We
>
> Jazz June.   We
> Die soon."

The students loved it. Every one of them. Major Mills . . . Vanella . . . Augusta . . . Critter . . . Jimmi-Jo . . . they all spoke up and asked for it again, and Miss Reeves read it again, until the class was reciting it along with her. Only then would they let her move on to another poem. The bell rang long before Mary-Larkin thought it was time.

All the classes were slow to get started, Mary-Larkin realized. Before third period that day she went to the library and checked out a book to read. She didn't bother to hide it during math or history class, just read it. If the class actually did something, she put the book away and took part, but when they were just killing time, as it seemed to her they did most of the time, she read.

As a matter of fact, she kept up the reading in class even after they got textbooks. English wasn't dull—Miss Reeves kept on reading lots of poetry and doing other interesting things—but the other classes were.

She noticed that Critter began to read in school, too, and sometimes they recommended books to one another, or swapped. Critter, she decided, was reading in junior high, instead of getting in trouble.

Chapter 12

The day of the seventh-grade assembly finally came.

Mary-Larkin was, as she put it to herself, really hyped up for it. She wore tights and a flared skirt and a turtle-neck knit top. She felt like she looked like a cheerleader, and her hopes were high. She was also very hungry by the time the assembly started.

She had talked to Missy and Callie and Sarah at Sunday school, and they had all assured Mary-Larkin that she would be a super cheerleader and that they knew she would win. She had in turn assured Missy and Callie that they were good and would get to be cheerleaders at Longstreet, and Sarah that she would get to be a cheerleader at the Christian Academy.

"Who knows if we'll even have cheerleaders," Sarah had said glumly. She was almost as sad about the Christian Academy as Mary-Larkin was about Wheatley. "We meet in the basement of the First Baptist Church," she said, "and it's moldy. We're going to have a fine new building on some land this man has donated. But I'll be in COLLEGE before that's built."

"At least even Wheatley has a new building," Mary-Larkin said.

"I guess," Sarah had said with a dreadful air of superiority, "it's not the buildings that count, but the *people*."

Mary-Larkin had ostentatiously turned to pay attention to the Sunday school teacher.

And now here it was time to go out on the stage at Phyllis Wheatley school and try out for cheerleader . . . the only white girl in the competition. What a funny way for her life to turn out!

Miss Horn called out the names, one by one, and each girl went out on the stage and led the two hundred or so seventh graders in a familiar yell.

If she just weren't so hungry, she thought, as she watched Vanella lead the group in "Go, Team, Go."

She was hungry because someone had stolen her lunch. She had set it down on the table where she always ate with Vanella and Augusta and Jimmi-Jo and gone up to the counter to get her milk. When she got back, her lunch was gone. "Who took it?" she asked. No one had seen anybody get it.

She had no money. She didn't really like to bring milk money to school, but her mother insisted. If she had no money, she could tell people that asked her for money that she had none, and they let her alone. Anyway, she drank her milk for lunch, and Vanella gave her a potato chip or two, and Augusta offered her half her apple. But it wasn't much of a lunch, and Mary-Larkin was hungry.

At last it was her turn, and she went out on the stage and looked at the audience. Goodness, a black audience was different from white audiences, she thought. You couldn't see the faces.

She said, with all the enthusiasm and pep she could summon, "All right, now, come on, let's do 'Hit 'em a lick.' "

She didn't trip over her own feet. She did a satisfactory job, and her leap at the end was the best she'd ever done. But she knew that she wasn't near as good as Vanella and some of the others. Still, she hoped. She thought of Critter, the token honky on the football team. Maybe they'd vote her the token honky cheerleader.

The election was conducted on the basis of applause for each contestant. Miss Horn and the football coach judged the volume of sound, as each girl stepped forward and the audience applauded according to the way they felt she had performed.

When Vanella Brasher's name was called, the sound was deafening. The reaction to the others varied. When it was Mary-Larkin's time to walk back on the stage, she was shocked at the tiny little sound of clapping that greeted her. But the worst thing was she heard a few hisses. That hurt. It was unbearable.

Covered with shame and embarrassment, Mary-Larkin fled backstage. She could see Miss Horn looking at her with sympathy.

"You did fine, baby," Vanella said.

But Mary-Larkin knew she hadn't. The winners' names were being called out, and Vanella and Lanett and the other winners went on stage to bow to the applause. They huddled, like a team, and broke and lined up across the stage and said, "All right, come on, gang, we're gonna do 'Soul! Soul.' "

Mary-Larkin couldn't stand it. To get the least amount of applause. To be *hissed*.

She ran from the auditorium, and though the school day was far from over, she went home.

At home her mother was typing furiously. Mary-Larkin ran into the room where she was and threw herself on the floor and sobbed.

"What's the matter?" Mrs. Thornhill said. "Mary-Larkin! What are you doing home from school?"

Mary-Larkin cried stormily.

"All right then, if you can't tell me what's the matter, I'll get on with my work," Mrs. Thornhill said, beginning to type again.

"You're cruel!" Mary-Larkin said. "You don't care what happens to me."

"Of course I care what happens to you," Mrs. Thornhill said. "But you know I can't tell what happens to you unless you stop crying and tell me."

"Oh, all right." Mary-Larkin stopped crying and told her mother about the cheerleader contest. "I was *humiliated*," she finished.

"Yes, I guess you did feel pretty bad," her mother said. "That's terrible."

Mary-Larkin began to cry again.

And Mrs. Thornhill began to type.

"See. You don't care," Mary-Larkin said.

"Of course I care. But I get bored listening to you cry. If you want to talk, I'll quit work and we'll talk. But don't just cry and cry."

Mary-Larkin sat up and looked at her mother.

"Okay," she said. "I wish I were dead."

Mrs. Thornhill got up and came over and sat on the

floor beside Mary-Larkin. "I don't wish you were dead," she said. "I'm terribly glad you're alive. Mary-Larkin, it's not the end of the world, you know."

"But I'll never get to be a cheerleader now," Mary-Larkin said.

"Is that so terrible? What's so great about being a cheerleader? I was astonished last spring when you said you wanted to be one in junior high."

"I know," Mary-Larkin sighed. "You never were a cheerleader in Wildflower and neither was Papa. You were both always reading good books and praying, I guess."

"Not absolutely every minute," Mrs. Thornhill said. "Come on, get up. Let's go downstairs. I'll fix you something warm and full of carbohydrates." Mrs. Thornhill paused. "Now I know that's the wrong thing to do, that all the rest of your life when the going gets rough, you'll want something rich and fattening." She sighed. "And for years I thought I was being such a good mother doing all that baking. . . ."

They went downstairs. "But, Mama, do you realize how awful it was? I got just a teeny bit of applause, and that was from Critter, I guess. And somebody hissed me. Hissed." Mary-Larkin began to whimper.

Mrs. Thornhill was pulling some frozen cookies out of the freezer. "Mary-Larkin, I don't know exactly what to say, and I hate for you to be unhappy, but can you imagine for a minute how some of those black children felt? Here you were, the little white girl up there trying out for cheerleader. They don't know you. But they probably sense you don't want to come to school there. They may resent you. And you said yourself that *all* the black girls were better than you were. Maybe they resented the fact that you got picked for the finals instead of another black girl. I don't know, but just chalk it up to experience. Learn from it."

"What can I learn?"

"You can learn that when you want something, you have to work very hard for it. Most of the time, anyway. Think through the goals you've set for yourself. Are they goals really worth the effort it will take to reach them? If they are, then work with everything you've got. If they're not, don't worry."

"Mama, you always moralize!"

"I don't mean to moralize," Mrs. Thornhill said. "I'm just trying to help you get some perspective."

"And now I'll get in trouble for leaving school without permission," Mary-Larkin said.

"I thought about that," Mrs. Thornhill said. "What do you think you'd better do?"

"I don't know," Mary-Larkin said. "Maybe they'll expel me. That would be super!"

They both laughed. "I guess I'll go with you tomorrow and see if everything is all right. Mr. Searle asked me to come by, anyway, to talk about the P.T.A. You know, a P.T.A. could do a lot of good things at Wheatley."

Chapter 13

Mary-Larkin had thought she could not possibly dread going to Wheatley school any more than she had the first few mornings, but she realized this morning that she could indeed be more afraid and more anxious.

She had never left school or skipped a class before in her life. What would they do to her? Would she be suspended?

Her head began to ache when she woke up. The ache was fierce and strong, like a vise tightened around her forehead.

"I can't go to school today, Mama," she said. "I have a headache."

"Mary-Larkin, are you sure you have a headache?"

"Yes, Mama, I'm sure." Mary-Larkin's headache was so bad she felt sorry for herself because her mother doubted that it was real.

"You know, headaches early in the morning are usually caused by tension, or—" Mrs. Thornhill broke off.

"I'm tense," Mary-Larkin said, "that's for sure."

In the end, Mary-Larkin took two aspirin and got in the car still feeling sorry for herself.

Mrs. Thornhill drove Critter and Mary-Larkin to school and went in with them. Everything looked just the same to Mary-Larkin. The kids were milling around the courtyard, sitting on the planters, leaning against the pillars as they always did. Nobody even looked at her. Nobody pointed at her and shouted, "Coward! Truant! Criminal!"

"I'll go on to homeroom," Mary-Larkin said, and Mrs. Thornhill hesitated, then nodded, and disappeared into the office.

In homeroom, Miss Reeves seemed especially nice to Mary-Larkin and nobody mentioned cheerleaders or assembly or anything else.

Miss Reeves, when homeroom was over and English class started, announced the class was going to start writing its own poetry.

Everybody groaned. "I can't write no poetry," Major Mills said.

"Sure you can," Miss Reeves said. "Take out a sheet of notebook paper." Notebooks dropped on the floor, and everybody took the opportunity to talk to a friend.

"All right, all right," Miss Reeves said. "Take a piece of notebook paper."

"Lend me a sheet of notebook paper," Major said to Mary-Larkin.

Mary-Larkin started to reach down to get her notebook on the shelf under her chair and then she said, "Major, you've got some notebook paper. Use your own."

Major grinned. "That's right, I do," he said. He took a sheet out of his notebook and smiled winningly at Mary-Larkin.

A few students had to borrow pencils. Mary-Larkin

71

went up to the front of the room to sharpen her own pencil. How on earth could they write poetry? she wondered.

"All right," Miss Reeves was saying. "Everybody have a sheet of notebook paper and pencil?"

Everybody said, yes, ma'am, they had paper and pencil.

"Now the big thing about poetry is *feeling*," Miss Reeves was saying. "All the poetry we've read together has been about feeling. Hasn't it?"

"That poem about the pool hall, 'We Real Cool,' " said Major, "what about that? Was that about feeling? That was about the dudes in the pool hall."

"Was it just a description of young men playing pool?" Miss Reeves asked. "Was that all it was?"

"No, ma'am," Vanella said.

"Why, Vanella?" Miss Reeves said.

"Because it made you sad about the dudes playing pool," Vanella said.

"That's right," Miss Reeves said. "You *felt*. You shared the sense of loss and waste with the poet, didn't you?"

The class hummed in agreement.

Mary-Larkin was always surprised at little Miss Reeves, whose voice was high and soft, the way she could always handle the class, even Major and the bad boys. She never seemed to get upset with them, almost never sent anybody to the office, but just quietly talked on and on and eventually everybody listened and nearly everybody understood what she meant.

And Miss Reeves could make you see something new

in the best way. It was exciting, Mary-Larkin thought. It was *feeling* that made poetry different from anything else. That's why it hit you so hard, she thought, if it hit you at all. It wasn't just facts . . . it was joy and gloom and despair and hope. . . .

Miss Reeves was going on with her instructions. "Take your piece of notebook paper and fold it down the middle, lengthwise, like this." She held up her own piece as a model.

Of course, as usual, there were a few students who insisted that they couldn't understand what Miss Reeves was talking about. They folded their paper crosswise, and the class waited until they got it right. It was at times like this in other classes that Mary-Larkin pulled out her book and read, but in Miss Reeves' class, the good part always came along pretty soon and she was afraid she'd miss something.

"All right," Miss Reeves said when they all had their paper folded right. "Now I want you to write on one side of the fold. Write down a description of something in this room. Write down the facts about it. Describe it as though you had to describe it in a letter to a person who had never seen it. Go ahead."

"What you mean?" several students asked, including Major.

"Here's an example," Miss Reeves said patiently. "The blackboard. Describe it. It's black. It's on the wall. It's about three feet tall and six feet long. It's flat. It's used to write on. Just describe one thing in the room that way. When you finish you can do another."

Most of the class began to write. A few sat there and

stared into space. Mary-Larkin had noticed that some of the black kids never did finish any of their work. What would happen to them? Would they fail English 7a? Miss Reeves moved over to a student who was just sitting there and began to talk softly to him. He finally began to write, and Miss Reeves moved to another.

Mary-Larkin wrote. She described the teacher's desk.

"A cube," she wrote. "Made of wood." She paused and thought. "It has sharp angles. It has drawers to store things. It is often locked. It's very neat."

Critter was writing furiously. He was on his third piece of paper. Major was writing slowly, painfully, but steadily. Vanella wrote fast, and then stopped. Jimmi-Jo was concentrating fiercely. Lanett was giggling with Wynona.

Mary-Larkin decided to go on and do something else besides the desk. She chose the window. "It is very tall and wide and the light shines through it so we can see. We never open the glass, though, because we have air conditioning. But on the other side I know the birds are singing and children are shouting. . . ."

"All right," Miss Reeves said. "Now, if you've finished, open your paper out and look down the other side. Write what you *feel* about the object you've described."

"What you mean, Teacher?" Major asked. "You mean, like my seat *feels* hard?"

Everybody roared with laughter, and Miss Reeves went right on. "You can write about how the thing in the room feels to you or you can write about how you feel about the thing in the room. . . . I thought it might be easier to write a poem if you write down how you feel about something."

Mary-Larkin thought. How did she feel about the teacher's desk? "I feel like the answers to everything are locked inside it," she thought. "If I had a desk, I could teach, too!"

She wrote that down, and felt exhilarated. It was like climbing the mountains in North Carolina—when you went to the top, you got a new view of the world. So this was how you wrote!

She moved to her description of the window.

"The window is a wall . . . that shuts out the world. . . ." she wrote. "I want to hear the children, and the birds . . . but I want to be in the classroom . . . safe and secure with light washing us. . . ." She wrote on.

"All right," Miss Reeves said, interrupting the class, some of whom were still writing, some of whom were talking. "See what you're written. Have you got the makings of a poem? Think about the poetry we've read together this year. It doesn't have to rhyme. See if you can make a poem out of what you've written. Hold up your hand if you need help, and I'll come."

Mary-Larkin pulled out a fresh piece of paper.

> The teacher's desk is forbidding,
> As secret as a safe,
> Behind it sits the teacher
> Keeping carefully the key.

Mary-Larkin looked at what she'd written. It sounded a little like a poem. It did. She felt another surge of excitement. It needed, though, a socko ending. How about. . . .

An apple for the teacher?
Would she trade it for the key?

"Very good, Mary-Larkin." Miss Reeves was standing beside her, reading what she'd written. "Listen to this, class. Mary-Larkin didn't use rhyme. She used another thing we find in poetry, though. Alliteration. You know, that's when you use a lot of words that begin with the same letter. 'As secret as a safe . . .' Hear the 'sssses'?"

Miss Reeves moved on, leaving Mary-Larkin feeling very pleased with herself. So she had used alliteration, had she?

"This is very good, Major," Miss Reeves said. "Listen class.

"The blackboard is black.
Blackboard is beautiful.
The blackboard is cool and hard and tough
 but the white chalk makes the marks on it.
Black is bigger and it lasts longer."

"Major is telling us something about being black, aren't you, Major? He's using symbolism. That's another thing you find in poetry. Very, very good, Major."

Major stood up and bowed to the class several times. The class applauded.

"I am a poet and don't know it," he said, laughing. "I am going to make a million dollars writing poetry."

"I hope you do, Major," said Miss Reeves, "and you can give all the credit to your dear old English teacher. . . ." She moved on to look at Vanella's work. "Vanella, this is very good. Vanella wrote about the blackboard, too.

> "The blackboard is big and square
> And I like to feel it up against my back
> But I hate to have to erase it
> And I hate to hear Major drag his
> fingernails across it."

Miss Reeves smiled at Vanella as the class laughed again because Major was once more bowing to acknowledge the attention he had gotten.

The period was over, almost before it had begun, Mary-Larkin thought.

Chapter 14

She had her first piano lesson of the year that afternoon and her mother picked her up at school.

"How's your headache?" Mrs. Thornhill asked.

Mary-Larkin was startled. She had completely forgotten her headache.

"Okay, I guess," she said.

"Good," Mrs. Thornhill said, "but just to be on the safe side I've made an appointment with Dr. Oglesby for Thursday afternoon to check your eyes."

"Okay," Mary-Larkin sighed gustily. For a minute, she forgot how much fun English class had been that morning and remembered only how horrible it had been when she had competed for cheerleader. Her head began to ache.

Her piano teacher was Mr. Maloney, a tall, thin, white-haired retired musician, who was, naturally, a member of the First Presbyterian Church.

Mr. Maloney asked her to play something for him. He listened and then said, "You didn't practice during the summer, did you?"

"No, sir," Mary-Larkin said.

"None of my pupils ever accomplished anything unless they practiced over the summer," Mr. Maloney said.

"I never will accomplish anything at the piano," Mary-Larkin said.

"You could if you wanted to," Mr. Maloney said. "Did you know that at one time in Vienna 90 percent of the people in town could play a musical instrument? Think of the music they made! What if 90 percent of the people in Stonewall could play an instrument?"

Mary-Larkin giggled. She had a mental picture of everyone in town playing an instrument, of Missy Cobb playing the flute, Miss Reeves a harp, Mr. Searle a big bass drum, her father the violin, and Critter—what could Critter play? The tuba, of course.

"So you're going to Wheatley this year?" Mr. Maloney was saying. "That's wonderful, Mary-Larkin. You know, you're a heroine! Your parents are wonderful people—they make all these other so-called liberals look like the hypocrites they are."

"Thank you, Mr. Maloney," Mary-Larkin said. It was wonderful that somebody—even old Mr. Maloney— thought she was a heroine.

Just the same, she thought, I'd rather not go to Wheatley.

That night, Mary-Larkin was standing in the library at home looking around.

"Don't we have anything but books about the Bible?" she asked. "And the Holy Land?"

"What are you looking for?" Mr. Thornhill asked her.

"Poetry," Mary-Larkin said.

"Poetry's up on the top shelf," Mrs. Thornhill said. "Get the little stepladder over there. Nobody's been reading much poetry around here lately. . . ." Her voice trailed off.

Mary-Larkin peered at the titles. Tennyson . . . Browning . . . Longfellow. Good grief, she thought, how antique could you get?

"What kind of poetry are you looking for," her mother asked.

"Miss Reeves has been reading some Gwendolyn Brooks to us," Mary-Larkin said, "and some Langston Hughes."

"Miss Reeves sounds like a superb English teacher," Mrs. Thornhill said. "I don't think we have any poetry that modern. Try some of the ones we used to call 'modern American poets.' I loved them in high school and college—Amy Lowell and Emily Dickinson and Edna St. Vincent Millay. Get down the Untermeyer anthology."

Mary-Larkin found the Untermeyer and took it down.

Her mother was still talking, ". . . and I liked Mr. Searle, too. He asked me to be on the program at the P.T.A., and your father, too."

Mary-Larkin caught her breath. "What did he say about me leaving school?" she asked.

"He just waved it away," Mrs. Thornhill said. "He said he knew there were bound to be a few problems during the 'transition.' He was sorry that some of the students acted in what he called an 'ungracious way.' We ended up apologizing to each other."

"Apologizing for what?"

"For centuries of racial isolation, I guess," Mrs. Thornhill said. "Anyway, it's all right. Don't worry about it."

"I'll never forget how horrible I felt when I heard them hiss," Mary-Larkin said.

"It's all over," Mrs. Thornhill said. "It's not easy to do new things, like integrate a school, Mary-Larkin. It's bound to get better. And it's a good school. You can tell Miss Reeves is a good English teacher."

"She sure is," Mary-Larkin said, "but they have good English teachers at Longstreet."

The next day, Mary-Larkin was walking home from school when Critter hurried to catch up with her.

"No football practice this afternoon," Critter said. "Teachers' meeting."

"Oh, that's right," Mary-Larkin said. "You know something, Critter? I just realized I'm not afraid to walk down Riggs any more. I don't even think about it."

"Me either," Critter said. "You know I kind of like going to this crazy school. I don't like being the low man on the football team, and I don't like them always asking me for money, but it's not so bad."

"Do they still ask you for money?" Mary-Larkin asked. "They don't bother me as much any more."

"I guess it's because you bring your lunch. I still buy my lunch," Critter said. "Are you coming to our seventh-grade football game Thursday?"

"I haven't been to any games," Mary-Larkin said.

"This is with Longstreet," Critter said.

"Oh, I don't think I want to go. I couldn't stand—"

Mary-Larkin broke off. She had been about to say she couldn't stand to see Missy being a cheerleader (she had become a cheerleader as easy as pie) while she, Mary-Larkin, sat in the stands with a bunch of black kids.

"You ought to come," Critter said.

"If I came, I'd sit on the Longstreet side with all my friends," Mary-Larkin said.

Critter looked at her in disgust. "Good grief, Wheatley's not that bad. We're taking part in the biggest social revolution this country's seen and those kids at Longstreet are sitting it out. We're where the action is."

"I want to sit it out," Mary-Larkin said.

"You're nuts," Critter said.

"Well, anyway, I have to go to the doctor Thursday afternoon to get my eyes checked so I can't go to the game," Mary-Larkin said.

"Oh," Critter said.

On Thursday afternoon, Mrs. Thornhill picked Mary-Larkin up in front of the school. The bus to take the seventh graders to the football game with Longstreet had not arrived, and a bunch of girls were clustered around the car when she got in.

"Why aren't you going to the game?" Augusta asked her.

"I have to go to the doctor," Mary-Larkin said, through the open car window.

"Are you pregnant?" Augusta asked.

"No," Mary-Larkin said. "No, I'm not." Some of the girls laughed, and Mrs. Thornhill and Mary-Larkin drove away.

"Why did she ask you if you were pregnant?" Mrs. Thornhill asked.

"I guess because that's about all they go to the doctor for," Mary-Larkin said. "Lots of the girls get pregnant. Some of them have babies—they bring them to the football games, they say."

"Good gracious," Mrs. Thornhill said. "In junior high."

Mary-Larkin felt a certain satisfaction in seeing her mother at last shocked by something that happened at Wheatley. She started to say that her own friend, Lanett, thought she was pregnant, but Mary-Larkin decided to wait until Lanett was sure.

They had to wait at the doctor's office and when she got in to see Dr. Oglesby, he took a long time with the examination.

"So you're going to Wheatley," Dr. Oglesby said.

"Yes, sir," Mary-Larkin said.

Dr. Oglesby shook his head sadly and looked at Mrs. Thornhill reproachfully. "I hope you know what you're doing," he said.

"We know what we're doing," Mrs. Thornhill said.

Dr. Oglesby said he found nothing at all wrong with her eyes, and advised her to take aspirin for her headaches.

Chapter 15

Wheatley activities began to dominate the Thornhill household by the middle of October.

Both Mr. and Mrs. Thornhill went to the first meeting of the P.T.A. and they came home to report that Mrs. Thornhill was the new president of the Phyllis Wheatley Junior High School P.T.A.

"How did that happen?" Mary-Larkin asked. "Weren't there any black parents there?"

"It was mostly black parents," Mr. Thornhill said. "Your mother was terrific."

"What did you do, Mama?" Mary-Larkin asked.

"For once I guess I said the right thing at the right time," Mrs. Thornhill said. "There were dozens of speeches. All the ministers from the Wheatley district were there—all of them black except your father—and each one of them made a speech. And they had a panel of teachers talk about what was expected from the P.T.A. And then a panel of students talked. And one of the students touched my heart. He said he hoped the P.T.A. would bring some cultural events to Wheatley because the students didn't have the money to go to things. And I was on a parents' panel and the speeches had gone on and on and when it was my time to speak I just said I volunteered to bring some cultural events to Wheatley and they clapped and elected me president of the new P.T.A."

"And you didn't even go to the P.T.A. at Millie Bybee," Mary-Larkin said.

"I know," Mrs. Thornhill said. "There wasn't anything you could do at Millie Bybee, anyway. This is different. We can change the world at Wheatley. But I've got to deliver the goods."

And she did deliver.

The P.T.A. got organized and adopted its bylaws, and the state president came to Stonewall to present Wheatley its charter and announced that it was the first *integrated* P.T.A. in the state.

Mrs. Thornhill then gave her full attention to bringing "cultural events" to Wheatley. She persuaded the Stonewall chamber music group to give a concert at the school. She talked the town's best painter and best sculptor into being "artists in residence" at Wheatley for a week. She got a brass group from the Atlanta Symphony to come down and perform.

She was on the phone constantly, except when she was holding a Wheatley meeting at the manse, or going out to a Wheatley meeting.

The Thornhill children were used to lots of meetings at home—they were all skilled at passing out ice-box cookies and serving coffee—but they had never seen anything like this.

"They're different from church meetings," Joe pointed out. "They don't pray."

"But there's so many of them," Luke said.

The P.T.A. made a difference at Wheatley—there was no doubt about that. And Mr. Searle loved the P.T.A. and the activities they sponsored. He loved introducing visiting performers, and he'd gladly rearrange the school schedule and have an assembly any day the P.T.A. produced an interesting visitor.

"Let's try to get Julian Bond," he said, "or Teddy Kennedy."

"Gosh," Mrs. Thornhill said. "Well, that's aiming high. I'll try."

She and Mrs. Kingsley organized some afternoon classes for students and their families in guitar playing and filmmaking.

They were especially proud of the filmmaking class and Mary-Larkin had to admit it was one of the most interesting things she'd ever done.

Critter said he wanted to come to filmmaking as soon as football season was over.

At the junior high fellowship at church one Sunday night, Mary-Larkin was talking to Missy and Callie and Sarah.

"Are you going to the Gadabouts' Christmas dance?" Missy asked Mary-Larkin.

The Gadabouts' dance at Christmas was a real dance at the country club. She and Missy had talked about it for hours during the long summer when they had sat on the porch roof trying to bleach their hair with lemon juice and sunshine.

It was the first dance for the girls of Stonewall, and they wore long dresses, and their mothers hired a real rock group. The girls "asked" boys but they didn't have real dates. The girls went in groups, chauffeured by their parents, and the boys arrived in their groups and met the girls at the dance. Mary-Larkin, living in a different world at Wheatley, had forgotten the Gadabouts.

"I don't know whether I'll go or not," she said. "I don't have anybody to ask."

"Ask Noble Paget. He still likes you. I know he does," Missy said.

"I might," Mary-Larkin said. "Who are you going to ask?"

"I've already asked Monk Stevens," Missy said.

"I'm going to ask Clyde Patterson," Callie said.

Sarah said she thought she'd ask a boy she'd met at the Christian Academy.

"Go ahead, go ask Noble," Missy said. "Right now."

"Not now," Mary-Larkin said.

She felt very uncomfortable around Noble Paget. She never saw him except at choir practice on Wednesday nights and on Sundays. And he went to Longstreet, when he lived in the Wheatley district.

"Mary-Larkin," said Callie, "you could ask a nigger boy."

Mary-Larkin felt her face flame. Missy looked shocked, and Sarah giggled.

It was the giggle that did it. "Well, I could do worse, I guess," Mary-Larkin said.

Now Sarah was shocked, as well as Callie and Missy.

"You shouldn't tease Mary-Larkin," Missy said. "She can't help it if—"

"If she's a nigger-lover like her parents?" Callie said.

"Callie!" Missy said. Mary-Larkin was silent. She was so mad she couldn't speak, or think.

"Well, she is a nigger-lover," Callie said. "Everybody

knows it. My daddy says her daddy is going to be thrown out of the church. He thinks it's awful the way the Thornhills run around with colored people all the time."

Mary-Larkin found her tongue. "My father's only doing what he knows is right!" she said. "Of course I go to a black school. And you ought to, too, Callie Hubbard. You're in the Wheatley district, just like I am. You gave a false address, and that's horrible. My parents would never tell a lie like that!"

"You think you're better than anybody else just because you're a nigger-lover!" Callie said.

Mary-Larkin got up and ran across the fellowship hall and went into the ladies' rest room. Missy came after her.

"Don't feel bad, Mary-Larkin," Missy said. "Callie is awful hateful sometimes."

Mary-Larkin began to cry, and it made her madder at herself than ever that she'd cry in front of Missy like this. "Oh, she makes me so mad," was all she could say.

"I know," Missy said. "You know how my folks feel about integration, but they would never let me say 'nigger.' I think it's just awful to say 'nigger.'"

"Not saying 'nigger' is just part of it," Mary-Larkin said. "The kids at Wheatley call each other 'nigger' all the time. But we can't call them 'nigger.'" She remembered the fight Joe and Luke had the first week of school and how they wouldn't call the little black boys 'nigger.' It was all so complicated. How could she explain it all to Missy? Integration was just too much—it mixed everything up.

Mary-Larkin splashed water on her face and went back for the rest of fellowship hour. She took part in all the games but did not look at Callie Hubbard.

Was it true? she wondered. Were people in the church mad at her father and mother because of Wheatley?

She started to ask her parents about it that night but she found it too hard to talk about. Or even think about.

Chapter 16

The next day when Mary-Larkin was about to get dressed for school, she flipped through the dresses hanging in her wardrobe.

Suddenly, she turned away from the wardrobe and went over to her chest of drawers and took out a pair of blue jeans.

She put on the jeans and a shirt and pulled on her tennis shoes. Then she gathered her books and went downstairs and got her breakfast and slid into a chair.

"Are you going to wear blue jeans to school?" Joe asked her.

"No dress code at Wheatley," Mary-Larkin said. She was waiting for her mother to send her back upstairs to change back into a dress.

"I always thought dress codes were silly," Mrs. Thornhill said. "Blue jeans are the most sensible garment for school I know of."

Her mother had surprised her again, Mary-Larkin thought. She had put on the blue jeans to sort of defy Callie and Missy and Sarah. Was it a commitment to

Wheatley? Rebellion against the establishment? What was it? Well, whatever it was, it made getting dressed in the morning a lot simpler.

Mary-Larkin fixed her lunch and went out front to wait for Critter and Mrs. Kingsley. Critter looked extraordinarily neat that morning, she thought. Or was it that she was just getting used to him?

She remembered what he'd said that afternoon on the way home from school: "Wheatley's where the action is." Suddenly, she decided she would confide in Critter.

When they got out at school, she did not hurry into the courtyard, but held back. "Critter, I want to talk to you," she said.

"Sure," he said.

And she told him about Callie and the ugly epithet, "nigger-lover."

Critter laughed. "You know, the kids all call me that in my neighborhood," he said. "And you know what I finally learned to say? I say, 'Yeah, I dig the jigs.' And that stops 'em cold!"

Mary-Larkin was impressed. Critter could be pretty cool. And he was only a Unitarian, too.

"Thanks," she said. "I may use that myself if I have the nerve."

"You're getting tougher all the time," Critter said. "I've been noticing. And I like your blue jeans."

They walked into the courtyard together, and Mary-Larkin joined Vanella and Jimmi-Jo and Lanett and Augusta by their own planter box.

"He your boyfriend?" Augusta asked for the one hundredth time.

91

"No," Mary-Larkin said, thinking again of Noble Paget. Noble Paget, who looked like Ashley Wilkes. Noble Noble Paget. What was so noble about Noble? she wondered. The bell rang, and she hurried up to Miss Reeves' room.

That night the Thornhills had company for supper. He was a reporter for the *New York Times* and his name was Paul Winfield. Mary-Larkin thought he was terribly good-looking.

He had come to Stonewall to do a story on its school integration and he had been referred right away to Mr. Thornhill. And Mr. Thornhill had invited Mr. Winfield home to supper and he had been happy to come.

"I eat in so many restaurants," he said to Mrs. Thornhill, as he presented her with a bottle of wine. "It's a pleasure to eat in a home again." He looked around him at the high ceilings, the old furniture, the books on the walls, and said, "Especially a home like this."

At the dinner table, he was full of praise for what he'd heard about Mrs. Thornhill's work with the Wheatley P.T.A. "It just shows what good things parents can accomplish in an integrated school," he said. "If they'll just work together. All those programs and special classes the P.T.A. has provided! They're wonderful."

A little later, he turned to Mary-Larkin. "How do you like going to Wheatley?"

"Okay, I guess," Mary-Larkin said. "I'd like to be in the school where all my friends go, but it's okay."

"I think it's wonderful what you and your family are doing," Mr. Winfield said. "But I've been wondering about something. Are you under any pressure from any of your white friends? Because you go to a black school,

I mean. I know a lot of your friends moved out of this neighborhood and gave false addresses. . . ."

Mary-Larkin hesitated. Was being called a nigger-lover pressure? "A little," she said finally.

"What kind of thing happens?" Mr. Winfield asked. He was persistent.

"Last night at church some of the kids called me a nigger-lover," Mary-Larkin said. That would serve Callie right, she thought, if it got printed in the *New York Times* that she had used a word like nigger-lover.

Mr. Winfield shook his head sadly. "What did you say when they called you that?" he asked.

"I didn't say anything at all," Mary-Larkin said. "I didn't know what to say. But now I know. I'll just say next time, 'Sure I dig the jigs.' That's what this boy at school told me to say."

Everybody—at least the grownups—laughed, and Mr. Winfield got out his little notebook and wrote something down in it.

Mrs. Thornhill asked Mr. Winfield if he had any children of his own.

He had two, he said, a boy and a girl.

"And where do they go to school?" Mrs. Thornhill asked him.

"They go to a really good private school," Mr. Winfield said. "The Bank Street School."

"They don't go to public school?" Mrs. Thornhill asked.

"No, public school is impossible in New York," Mr. Winfield said. "We were lucky to get them in Bank Street School."

Mr. and Mrs. Thornhill had both stopped eating and

were looking at Mr. Winfield. Mary-Larkin watched him, too. Joe and Luke kept eating.

"Why?" asked Mrs. Thornhill. "Why is public school impossible in New York?"

"It's just not safe," Mr. Winfield said.

"Why?" Mr. Thornhill asked.

"Why what?" Mr. Winfield said, puzzled.

"Why isn't it safe?"

"Oh, you know. The crime rate. It's just not safe." He looked from one to the other of the Thornhills, and he added, "It has nothing to do with race. Nothing. Bank Street School is integrated. It has *nothing*, I tell you, to do with race."

Mrs. Thornhill smiled briefly. "One of the few things that really discourages me about the future of this country is that everybody we know in Washington and New York is all for integration and applauds what we're doing in Stonewall—but every one of them sends his own children to private school."

"I just can't take a chance with my own children," Mr. Winfield said.

Mary-Larkin remembered her first day at Wheatley and how scared she'd been. But nothing had happened to her, not really. They had "borrowed" her lunch money, and one boy had done something to Annette, but surely anybody could see it wasn't really any more dangerous at Wheatley than it was at Longstreet. And if all her friends had been at Wheatley like they were supposed to be, then she wouldn't have ever been scared.

The grownups were chatting about the whole civil rights battle across the South, which Mr. Winfield had covered for the *New York Times* for several years.

Mary-Larkin wanted to point out to him that if *everybody* went to public school in New York, then it would be a lot safer, but she didn't want to interrupt the grownups.

She did try to talk about it with her mother later that night.

"You're absolutely right," Mrs. Thornhill said. She hugged Mary-Larkin. "I knew you had good sense."

"Mama, are some of the people in the church mad at Daddy and you about Wheatley?"

"There's been a little grumbling," Mrs. Thornhill said. "But I don't think there's a really strong objection. Your father is a really good minister, you know, Mary-Larkin. And the people know that. He's a good preacher, and he's a good administrator, and he works hard, and he visits, and he's conservative enough for even Stonewall on everything but race."

She paused and looked thoughtful. "You know, they got mad at me about the swimming pool, when I went down to the city council. But they got over that. I don't think there'll be any real trouble in the church for your father. He's on sound theological ground, you know."

Mary-Larkin felt only slightly reassured.

Chapter 17

"Why don't you ever bring any friends home after school?" Mrs. Thornhill asked Mary-Larkin.

"I don't know," Mary-Larkin said. Her mother asked her that question nearly every day, it seemed, and Mary-Larkin had thought about asking Vanella to come home with her. Vanella, in lots of ways, was like Missy Cobb. They were both pretty and cute and popular. Both were social leaders in their class, and neither was terribly interested in schoolwork.

She liked Missy, and she liked Vanella. Both were naturally warm and friendly. Vanella had been friendly to her from the first day of school—when she had really needed a friend—and Mary-Larkin would always remember it with gratitude.

But somehow, she couldn't imagine Vanella coming home with her, walking down Riggs, crossing Broad, coming down Church Street. She just couldn't.

Vanella never mentioned her father, but he didn't live with them. Her mother worked as a nurse's aide at the hospital. While the Thornhills thought of themselves as poor, when they compared themselves with other members of the Presbyterian church, Vanella was poor in a different way.

There was simply no money for anything but bare necessities in Vanella's home. She had to wait to pay her art fee until her mother got paid. And the art fee was only $1.50. Vanella had never owned a book in her life. Vanella didn't care that she didn't own a book, but it worried Mary-Larkin.

One morning it was too rainy to stay in the courtyard until the bell rang and Mary-Larkin went on up to homeroom, and talked to Miss Reeves.

For some reason they got to talking about the money situation for the kids at Wheatley, and Mary-Larkin mentioned to her that Vanella had no books.

"I know," Miss Reeves said, and she shook her head. "They don't have anything they can call their very own. I have a friend who's a social worker and she explained to me that that's why the girls want to have babies. It's something of their very own, a baby. They won't have abortions, you know, if they get pregnant."

Mary-Larkin thought of Lanett, who was thirteen, and pregnant. Would Lanett be happy to have a baby of her very own? She had certainly not seemed to be very upset about being pregnant.

But partly because of this vast difference in family income between her and the Wheatley girls, she never felt at ease with them. She liked Augusta and Lanett and Vanella and Jimmi-Jo, but never felt able to say, "Come home with me this afternoon."

And then Mary-Larkin began to notice Jimmi-Jo more.

97

Jimmi-Jo was the quietest girl in their class, and so had attracted very little attention from Mary-Larkin. But as the weeks passed, Mary-Larkin couldn't help but see that Jimmi-Jo was very good at her schoolwork, and that she liked to read.

Mary-Larkin and Critter Kingsley went to the school library nearly every day to check out a new book. Jimmi-Jo soon began to go with them. The three of them were the pride and joy of Miss Phifer, the librarian. Miss Phifer held them up as models for the other students. "The rest of you just come in the library to play checkers and dominos," she said, "but Crichton and Jimmi-Jo and Mary-Larkin *read!*"

Mary-Larkin and Jimmi-Jo began to eat lunch together, still sitting at Vanella's table, but always sitting down at one end and chatting together instead of always joining in the general conversation.

Jimmi-Jo had just moved to Stonewall, it turned out, and so she felt almost as much an outsider at Wheatley as Mary-Larkin. It was funny, Mary-Larkin thought, how much everybody looked alike and seemed alike until you got to know them. And then when you really knew them, they were as different as they could be. Who would have thought that Jimmi-Jo was new?

They became friends, and one day, Mary-Larkin asked Jimmi-Jo to come home after school with her the next day. Jimmi-Jo said she'd ask her mother and let her know. The next day, she said it was fine.

After school, the two of them walked down Riggs and crossed Broad and turned off on Church and walked to the manse.

Jimmi-Jo looked around her as they went up the front

steps and crossed the porch. Inside, she stood quite still and looked around some more.

Mrs. Thornhill came out of the kitchen and greeted them enthusiastically. In fact, Mary-Larkin felt that her mother was entirely too enthusiastic. But I guess she's so proud of me for bringing home a black girl she's about to pop, she told herself.

Mrs. Thornhill had made brownies and Mary-Larkin and Jimmi-Jo took a handful apiece and went upstairs to Mary-Larkin's room.

There were a few uneasy moments while Mary-Larkin worried about what to do for the whole afternoon, but there was no problem. Jimmi-Jo looked at all Mary-Larkin's books and then they looked at magazines together. They gave each other psychological tests out of the women's magazines: "Are You Ready for Marriage?" and "Are You Yin or Yang?"

When it was time for Jimmi-Jo to leave, they went downstairs. Mrs. Thornhill volunteered to take Jimmi-Jo home. "I'll have to hurry though," she said. "We've got to get back to the church for supper and you have choir practice. . . . If I can find my keys. . . ."

"Do you sing in the choir?" Jimmi-Jo asked her.

"The Youth Choir at our church," Mary-Larkin said.

"I'll bet that's fun!" Jimmi-Jo said.

"It is, kind of," Mary-Larkin said, surprised. She'd always taken the church choirs for granted. She had been enrolled in the Cherub Choir when she was six, and had gone into the Junior Choir when she went into fourth grade, and now, automatically, she was in the Youth Choir.

"Do you like to sing, Jimmi-Jo?" Mrs. Thornhill

99

asked, moving the cushions on the sofa and looking under them.

"Yes, ma'am," Jimmi-Jo said. "I sure do. We had a chorus in the elementary school I went to in Nashville. But I couldn't take music here."

"Why?" Mary-Larkin asked. She began to help Mrs. Thornhill look for her car keys.

"I don't know," Jimmi-Jo said. "I never could understand what the counselor was saying."

"I know," Mary-Larkin said, and they exchanged looks of sympathy . . . they shared bewilderment at what authority was talking about, the common lot of all junior high school students.

Mrs. Thornhill was back in the kitchen now, looking on the counter tops and in the cabinets and even in the oven.

"Maybe they're in the car," Mary-Larkin said.

"What about your church choir, Jimmi-Jo?" Mrs. Thornhill said. "Can't you sing in your church choir?"

"We don't go to church," Jimmi-Jo said.

That was like waving a red flag at a bull, Mary-Larkin thought. Now her mother would never stop. "Then you must come with Mary-Larkin and join our choir! If you like to sing, you just come and sing! Can you go to supper at the church with us and go to choir practice tonight?"

"I'll have to call my mama," Jimmi-Jo said.

"Call her," Mary-Larkin said.

Mrs. Thornhill found her car keys and announced loudly she was putting them in her purse as soon as she could find her purse.

"It's okay," Jimmi-Jo said. "I can go."

"Oh, good," Mary-Larkin said. But deep down inside, Mary-Larkin was a little bit sorry. And she was sorry she was sorry, but choir practice had given her another chance to see her old friends like Missy and Callie and Sarah and even Noble Paget—if only from a distance.

She liked Jimmi-Jo, but she was an alien presence, and Mary-Larkin dreaded, among other things, all the introductions she'd have to make.

Mrs. Thornhill rounded up Joe and Luke, and Mary-Larkin and Jimmi-Jo went upstairs to freshen up. Mary-Larkin combed her hair, and Jimmie-Jo patted hers.

They all walked over to the church together, and Mr. Thornhill waved at them from across the fellowship hall where dinner was being served.

At the little table where old Mr. Apple was collecting money, Mrs. Thornhill paid for "four students and two adults" and they all got in line at the counter where the members of the Klesis Circle were serving supper. Everybody in the line seemed to get awfully quiet. The Klesis were great cooks, and when it was their time to serve the Wednesday night supper at the church, the food was always good. Sure enough, tonight they had fixed chicken and dumplings.

The Klesis ladies—all white-haired since Klesis was the oldest circle in the First Presbyterian Church of Stonewall—had been chattering to the people in the line ahead of the Thornhills, but when Mrs. Thornhill and the Thornhill children and Jimmi-Jo got to the counter, the Klesis ladies got quiet and served the food and passed the plates in a hurry.

101

The Thornhills picked up silver and made their way to a table where there were some empty places. Luke and Joe sat down and began to eat. Mrs. Thornhill said, "Look, Mary-Larkin, you and Jimmi-Jo can sit over there by Callie and Missy if you want to. . . ."

Mary-Larkin led Jimmi-Jo over and she introduced her to Missy and Callie, as they were laying their plates down and arranging their silver and getting settled.

Callie got up and left. Apparently she hadn't been very hungry.

"You must go to Wheatley," Missy said to Jimmi-Jo.

At least Missy was being decent, Mary-Larkin thought.

"Yes," Jimmi-Jo said, and did not utter another word. Mary-Larkin remembered how quiet Jimmi-Jo had been at school until she'd gotten to know her.

She wished Jimmi-Jo would talk more, and she wished Callie hadn't called her a nigger-lover, and she felt self-conscious having a black girl as a guest in the all-white crowd in the fellowship hall. But she shouldn't feel that way, she realized. She shuddered.

"What's the matter with you?" Missy asked her.

"Nothing," Mary-Larkin said. "I just shivered."

"I hope you're not catching a virus," Missy said. "If you are, don't give it to me." She jumped up and took her dirty dishes to the counter.

Mary-Larkin tried to think of something to say to Jimmi-Jo and couldn't. Jimmi-Jo, of course, said nothing. Mary-Larkin ate. "As soon as we finish, we'll go to the choir room. We have a good choir—I guess," she said finally.

"Do you all sing at church services?" Jimmi-Jo asked.

"We sing at the early service every Sunday," Mary-Larkin said. "Our church building is old and small and we have two Sunday services even though our congregation isn't all that big."

They were through eating and got up. Mrs. Thornhill waved at them, and Mary-Larkin waved back. As they walked across the fellowship hall with their dirty dishes, Mary-Larkin felt a wave of silence, heated with stares, following them. She felt conspicuous, and she felt miserable, and she hated it because Jimmi-Jo, not being a fool, must sense that her presence was causing comment, or rather causing that dreadful no-comment silence.

Whatever happened to the Brotherhood of Man? Mary-Larkin wondered, the oneness of God's church?

Jimmi-Jo followed her trustingly down to the Youth Choir room and they sat down. Mr. McLeod, the choir director, came hurrying in and looked inquiringly at them, and Mary-Larkin introduced Jimmi-Jo and told him Jimmi-Jo liked to sing.

Mr. McLeod couldn't have been nicer. "Welcome," he said. "We need good voices. Are you a soprano or an alto?"

As the other kids came drifting in, each one seemed to stop and stare at Mary-Larkin and Jimmi-Jo.

Good grief, don't they have some black kids at Longstreet and Lee? Mary-Larkin wondered. What's such a big deal about this? She was becoming angry at the kids in the choir.

At the beginning of every choir practice, Mr. McLeod

103

let them warm up by singing a few songs that the choristers chose themselves.

"What'll it be tonight?" Mr. McLeod asked, standing before them with his hand on his music rack.

Several voices piped up with "Amazing Grace," and the accompanist started playing it. The choir's voices rose and Mary-Larkin began to sing:

> "Amazing grace—how sweet the sound—
> That saved a wretch like me!
> I once was lost, but now am found,
> Was blind, but now I see."

The members of the choir had been so delighted when Arlo Guthrie had sung a song that was in the Presbyterian *Hymnbook* in *Alice's Restaurant* that it had become their favorite song.

The words of the third verse struck Mary-Larkin as rather appropriate:

> "Through many dangers, toils, and snares,
> I have already come;"

She had indeed come through many "dangers, toils, and snares" since school had started the day after Labor Day.

> "Tis grace has brought me safe thus far,
> And grace will lead me home."

Mary-Larkin wasn't sure exactly what "grace" meant, but Papa was always preaching about it, and it was supposed to be readily available. Maybe there was something to the God bit, and maybe grace would see her through the "dangers, toils, and snares" that lay ahead.

I certainly hope something will, Mary-Larkin thought.

As they sang, Mary-Larkin noticed that Jimmi-Jo could truly sing, and for a twelve-year-old girl, her voice was something else. She stopped singing to listen, and was impressed.

Mr. McLeod walked around the room and came and stood close to Jimmi-Jo and beamed like he'd stumbled on a diamond mine in his own backyard.

When they finished "Amazing Grace," Mr. McLeod looked up for requests, and Mary-Larkin, to her horror, heard a voice cry out, "Old Black Joe." She was sure it was malicious mischief on somebody's part, to insult Jimmi-Jo. Mr. McLeod ignored the request and Mary-Larkin quickly yelled out, "They'll Know We Are Christians by Our Love!" and Mr. McLeod nodded and said, "That's a good one," and the accompanist began to play it.

When they got down to work on the anthem for Sunday you could tell that Mr. McLeod was very, very pleased with Jimmi-Jo. When choir practice was over, he asked her to stand up and he introduced her to the choir, and said, "Now each one of you stand up and tell your name, so Jimmi-Jo will know you," he said. Everybody did it, and afterward, several young people came over and told Jimmi-Jo they were glad to have her, just the way they would have done a white newcomer. Missy came over, but Callie and Sarah didn't. Neither did Noble.

Mary-Larkin and Jimmi-Jo walked across to the manse, and Mr. Thornhill took Jimmi-Jo home. (Mr. Thornhill *always* knew where his car keys were, and Mrs. Thornhill had, unbelievably, lost hers again.)

"I'm glad you brought a friend to choir practice," Mr.

Thornhill said on the way home. "Will she come back?"

"I don't know," Mary-Larkin said. "She sings good."

"I hope she comes back," Mr. Thornhill said.

"Papa, I don't understand Christians," Mary-Larkin said.

"What do you mean?"

And Mary-Larkin poured out all her resentment and confusion. Why had people who professed to be Christians lied about their addresses rather than go to a black school? Why did somebody who professed to be a Christian call her a nigger-lover? Why would somebody in a church choir deliberately ask for "Old Black Joe" when a black girl was visiting the choir?

"That was a terrible thing to do," Mr. Thornhill agreed; but then he warned Mary-Larkin about the sin of pride. "Civil rights is so important to us—your mother and me and you children, too—that we tend to judge everybody on how they react to integration. And it is important—of course, it's important. But there are other sins besides racism. And it's very wicked for us to congratulate ourselves on our tolerance and then condemn other people as racists. Don't judge people until you've stood in their shoes. It's easy for you, since you have parents who believe in integration, but for Missy, whose parents are segregationists—"

"Missy's better than a lot of 'em," Mary-Larkin said. "And at least they moved; they didn't lie about where they lived. And it's not easy for me to be tolerant. How can you think it's easy?" She was sobbing now. "It's the hardest thing I've ever done—to be a liberal. I want to be popular! I just want to go to Longstreet with my friends!"

"I shouldn't have said it was easy," Mr. Thornhill said. "It's never easy to do what's right."

By this time they were back at the manse, and Mr. Thornhill had turned off the ignition. He reached over and took her hand.

Mary-Larkin squeezed his hand, and then struggled out of the car.

Mr. Thornhill walked around the car and put his arm around her. "Remember Abraham and Isaac, and how hard it was for Abraham to do what God told him to do. But how right it was—"

Mary-Larkin jerked away from him. "Oh, you always have to bring up something out of the old *Bible!*"

She ran in the side door and Mr. Thornhill followed her inside.

"Isn't life interesting right now?" he said. "Aren't your horizons widening? Don't you know more about the world than you did?"

"I sure do," Mary-Larkin said and ran upstairs.

Chapter 18

Life moved on.

Mary-Larkin realized that things just never stood still.
She went to school. She ate lunch with Jimmi-Jo.
Jimmi-Jo came home with her every Wednesday afternoon, and they ate supper at the church and then went to choir practice.

Jimmi-Jo began to come on Sunday morning to sing in church with the Youth Choir but she did not stay for Sunday school.

Mary-Larkin enjoyed Jimmi-Jo, but just the same, she felt now a little more isolated from Missy and Callie and Sarah and Noble and the others.

Still, at Missy's urging, she called up Noble Paget and invited him to the Gadabouts' dance. He accepted and thanked her.

At school, she had to admit things were getting more and more interesting. More and more people were coming to Wheatley to write articles about the "integrated school in Stonewall," although it wasn't all that integrated, Mary-Larkin thought.

But the P.T.A. was so active and brought so many new things to the school—a puppet theater group, a weaver who taught everybody how to make a box loom, a black sculptor, and a wonderful lady who talked about black people in history and told tales of Sojourner Truth and the black jockey who won the first Kentucky Derby and the black Arctic explorer.

Another lady came and showed them some African folk dances and there was talk of a Swahili course for everyone. Black heritage became a common phrase.

Jimmi-Jo quit straightening her hair and came to school with a "natural."

"Nobody but white people call it an Afro," Mary-Larkin explained to her mother.

A lot of classes continued to be dull, but never English, where Miss Reeves drilled them on grammar and other essentials of life for two days a week and then went back to poetry reading and poetry writing for three days.

Between the books that Mary-Larkin was reading during math and history and French classes and the poetry she was reading at home and at school, her head was always buzzing with new images and ideas and figures of speech, and tag ends of lines like "Christ, what are patterns for?" and "It makes a lovely light," and "I think it must be lonely to be God."

Seventh-grade football was over in November, and Critter began coming to filmmaking class after school. He loved it, and when he found a poem, "The Camera," in a book he checked out of the library, he was beside himself with excitement. "Listen!" he said, and read it out loud to Miss Reeves:

"Light disperses the silver
On film in the darkness
And memory is trapped. . . ."

"If I could write a poem like that!" he said.

"You can," Miss Reeves assured him.

One afternoon during filmmaking class a tall black man came into the library where Mike, the film instructor, was showing them how to use a splicer.

"Here you are," the man shouted, "learning the white man's thing." He wore a broad-brimmed hat, and a dashiki, and his eyes raked the black kids in the room.

The kids looked at him, black and white both bewildered. Mike, who was white and had long hair and wore sandals, seemed as puzzled as anybody else.

But as the black man began to speak again, it was Mike who said quietly, "Hey, man, this is every man's thing. How are black kids going to make black movies unless they learn how?"

He turned back to his pupils and the splicer and the class went on, with everyone ignoring the "dude," who soon strolled out.

On the way home, Critter and Mary-Larkin talked about the visit.

"Who was he?" Mary-Larkin wondered.

"Oh, some man up there in the black neighborhood, I guess. Maybe he's into the Panthers or something," Critter said.

"The Black Panthers? Right here in Stonewall?" Mary-Larkin asked.

"Right here in River City," Critter said. "I bet they have a Panthers group here."

"They have N.A.A.C.P.," Mary-Larkin said. "My father belongs."

"So do my parents," Critter said.

"And Jimmi-Jo's father," Mary-Larkin said. "He's a doctor."

"But the N.A.A.C.P. is not the same thing as the Panthers," Critter said loftily.

"I know that," Mary-Larkin said.

One day the P.T.A. brought a black poet to visit English classes at Wheatley. When he came bounding into Miss Reeves' class early one morning, he reminded Mary-Larkin a little of the black man who had come into film-making.

He said his name was Wayne Odell but he had changed it to Ngoma, which means music and dancing in Swahili.

He brought with him a record player, some records, a slide projector, and Aubrey Little followed him into the room carrying a screen.

Ngoma was thin and terribly energetic and lively. He never stood still. He wore a beard and a denim cap, high-heeled shoes and knit turtleneck shirt. He moved about, even while Miss Reeves was introducing him.

"He's a graduate student at the State University," she said. "And he's a writer. His poems have been published in real magazines. And he's going to help us with our poetry writing."

Ngoma began to set up his equipment and while he was doing it, he talked. "We're going to have lots of fun," he said. "We're going to write us some poetry."

As he moved around, putting up the screen, setting up the projector, adjusting the record player, his heels clicked and clacked on the bare classroom floor.

The students were interested in him—there was no doubt of that. His vitality seemed to be seeping into them, too. Major was sitting up straight and watching Ngoma very closely.

"Yeah, man," Ngoma said, "we are going to write some cool poetry. Miss Reeves here told me you all are really turned on to poetry. More than any other class. Okay, man, let's see what we can do!"

He became very serious. "Poetry comes through experience," he said. "It's nice to see how people see a thing differently. And then they communicate what they see to other people.

"Now here's one way to write a poem."

He began to write on the blackboard:

VISUALIZE
REMEMBER THE VISUALIZATION
PUT IT ON PAPER
PUT IT IN ORDER
PUT IT IN FORM

"You can put it in poetry form," Ngoma said, "or you can put it in free style. Free style is just what it sounds like. Free. In college, they start talking about meters and iambic and all that. And it gets kind of boring. Just remember that the British soldiers walked in straight ranks and they got ripped off because they couldn't break ranks. Poetry style is like the British and free style is like the Americans.

112

"You should have the pleasure of writing the way you want to. It's *yours*. Nobody can take that away from you."

Ngoma dusted his hands to get the chalk dust off, and said, "Now you gonna see some slides come up here on the screen. I want you to write down what you see in the slides. Just put down on paper what comes into your mind as you look at the slides . . . it may be things like love . . . joy . . . happiness . . . whatever. . . ."

Miss Reeves turned out the classroom lights and the slides began to pop up on the screen.

There were colored photographs of civil rights demonstrations, of overflowing garbage cans, of black children playing in a park, black people embracing Martin Luther King, Jr.

The record began to play trumpet music as the slides clipped on and off.

Mary-Larkin began to write furiously, trying to write down everything she thought of as the slides continued— Stokely Carmichael, black old people sitting in rocking chairs, and on and on.

"What'd you write down?" Ngoma asked when the slide show was over, the lights back on, the music quiet.

The students began to call out things—"sadness . . . black people . . . angry people . . . hip . . . friendly . . . important . . . police . . . Stokely . . . violent."

"Okay, that's good," Ngoma said. "Now write a poem using some of those ideas."

Some of the students began to write and others tapped their pencils on their desks. Mary-Larkin was writing furiously, writing as if to save her life by writing poetry as fast as she could, overwhelmed with ideas she wanted to get down.

She scratched out and wrote again and finally copied her poem over:

> Sunshine out of doors
> Young people and a baby
> With beads and braids
> African colors and nailheads
> Frizzy hair
> Sunshine and death
> Drums and smoke
> Drums and sunshine
> Smiles and earrings
> Shades and sunshine
> Babies and love
> Up against the wall
> Corn rows and sad black faces
> Oh, my brothers, and oh, my sisters,
> Do not hate me so!

Ngoma took up the poems the students had written and promised to come back in a few days. He began to take down his equipment when the bell rang.

Chapter 19

Ngoma came back, as promised, on a Wednesday.

"You are all poets," he announced. "Each and every one of you is a poet, and don't let anybody tell you any different."

He shuffled through some of the papers he held in his hands. "This is the class that's really turned on to poetry," he said. "You can tell you all are poetry freaks, all right."

Ngoma wore another cap and a flowered shirt this time. "I want to read some for you. Listen to this one. It has power," he said, and he read Major Mills' poem, which was full of four-letter words and how bad white people had been to black people.

"I want to show you how two different people can feel different ways about the same thing," he said, and he read Mary-Larkin's poem. He read it carefully, and when he came to the last two lines, he read them so that they sounded sadder than death:

> "Oh, my brothers, and oh, my sisters,
> Do not hate me so!"

115

The class was quiet.

Ngoma laid the paper down. "She wrote about what she feels, like I said," he said. "It's written from the heart." He paused, and corrected himself. "No, it's written from the soul."

He looked at Mary-Larkin. "It's written from the soul, Sister. And we don't hate you, Sister. It just takes a little while and we'll all be poets together. You'll see, Sister."

Mary-Larkin felt as though she were in a very holy place, more holy than church.

She wanted to cry, and she wanted to laugh.

Then she felt a touch on her shoulder—Jimmi-Jo, who sat across the aisle, had reached over and patted her shoulder. Vanella turned around and smiled at her.

Ngoma Odell gathered up his papers, almost dancing toward Miss Reeves to hand them to her.

"Here's all their poems," he said. "Not quite all of them. I'm gonna enter some of them in a poetry contest for high school kids. Some of you all may be famous." He grinned and bowed and hurried out of the room, not even waiting to listen to Miss Reeves' thank-yous.

That afternoon, Critter walked home with Mary-Larkin and Jimmi-Jo and heard about the Youth Choir at the Presbyterian church.

"Can a Unitarian come?" he asked.

"The choir sings on Sunday mornings at the early service," Mary-Larkin said. "Don't you have to go to the Unitarian church?"

"I guess I do," Critter said, disappointed. "My family would have to be Jewnitarians."

116

"What are Jewnitarians?"

"That's what Harry Golden calls Unitarians," Critter said. "We think it's funny."

Jimmi-Jo said, with unusual force, that she hated Jews.

Critter and Mary-Larkin both turned on her. "How can you be anti-Semitic?" Critter demanded. "Jews have been the leaders in the civil rights movement."

"But they've cheated black people for years," Jimmi-Jo insisted.

"Oh, come on," Critter said. "If a few Jewish storekeepers charged high prices in your neighborhood, does that mean all Jewish people are bad?"

"No, of course not," Jimmi-Jo said. "Oh, I know you're right. But I like to look down on a few people myself."

"I know," Mary-Larkin said, "everybody has to have somebody to kick around."

"You know," Jimmi-Jo said, "you all think you're so fine and liberal and all, but you say things that make me want to—I don't know—hit you, I guess."

"What?" Mary-Larkin said. "What do you mean? What did I say?"

Critter stopped and stared at Jimmi-Jo and waited.

"I guess you don't mean anything by it," she said in a voice rising with anger, "but just now, Critter, you said something about 'your neighborhood.' Well, my neighborhood is just as good as your neighborhood! I get tired of the way you look down on us."

"But we don't—" Mary-Larkin began.

"Oh, yes, you do," Jimmi-Jo said. "You think you

don't. You think you're so nice. But you are always saying things like 'disadvantaged' when you mean black. And one time Critter said to me, 'If you weren't a black chick, I'd take you out.' "

"I was just making a joke!" Critter roared. "I don't care if you're black—or purple. I wouldn't take anybody out—I mean, I'm not even allowed to have dates yet! I was just being funny. I thought."

"Well, it wasn't very funny to me," Jimmi-Jo said.

"And you—" she turned to Mary-Larkin. "You won't hardly even speak to Major Mills or any of the black guys."

"I do!"

"You act like you're better than they are."

"I do the best I can," Mary-Larkin said. "I don't know how to act around boys anyway."

"I didn't know girls ever felt like that," Critter said thoughtfully.

"Listen, Jimmi-Jo," Mary-Larkin said. "Please. I wouldn't want to hurt you for anything. If I say something that sounds bad, I don't mean it to sound bad. I mean, you have to be patient."

Jimmi-Jo, quiet little Jimmi-Jo, who had been a whirling tornado there for a minute, was becoming her old self.

"I'm sorry I hollered at you all," Jimmi-Jo said. "I guess it was just the nigger in me coming out."

Mary-Larkin and Critter roared with laughter. The relief was exquisite.

"Listen, Jimmi-Jo, you'll have to tell us when we do wrong," Critter said. "My mom was telling about this book she read by a woman in Virginia who wanted to get to know black people and she had to take lessons in how to talk from a black newspaperman. At first, everything she said was wrong—no matter how hard she'd try, she'd say something that had a double meaning or something. I'm glad you yelled at us. We like you. I like going to Wheatley. I want integration to work."

"I know," Jimmi-Jo said. "It gets better the more we are together. That's what that cat Ngoma said."

"It sure does," Mary-Larkin said.

They walked on in companionable silence, until Critter turned off and left them.

When they got to the manse, Mrs. Thornhill was nowhere to be seen and there were no brownies or Tollhouse or even ice-box cookies in the kitchen.

"Mama must have *died*," Mary-Larkin said.

They made peanut-butter sandwiches and they were taking them upstairs when Mrs. Thornhill came in the side door. She looked worried.

"Hi, Mama, what's the matter?"

"Nothing much," Mrs. Thornhill said. "How are you two girls today?"

"Just fine," they said and went on upstairs. They looked at magazines and talked about school and the books they were reading, but Mary-Larkin was uneasy.

When they all went over to the church for supper, Mary-Larkin saw her mother and father having a brief, tense discussion in a corner of the fellowship hall.

She and Jimmi-Jo finished supper and went to choir practice. Mr. McLeod had a new anthem for them to learn—and it had a solo part for Jimmi-Jo.

119

Mary-Larkin did not get a chance to talk to Missy or Callie or anybody that night.

The next day in the school lunchroom, Mary-Larkin told Vanella and the others about Jimmi-Jo's solo part in the anthem the Youth Choir was working on.

They had talked about choir practice before at lunch, but now Vanella was transfixed with the idea of Jimmi-Jo's solo.

"Can the rest of us sing in your choir?" Vanella asked.

"Sure you can," Mary-Larkin said. Well, why not? she wondered.

Augusta and Lanett, who was still in school, though getting plump, wanted to come. Beverly said she might want to, too.

That night at supper, Mary-Larkin said, "Hey, everybody at school wants to join our choir. On account of Jimmi-Jo's solo, I guess. Shall I tell them to come to the church for supper, or after supper?"

"How many?" Mr. Thornhill asked.

"Well, three or four said they wanted to come. It probably won't be but one or two when it comes right down to it."

"Should she ask them to wait a while?" Mrs. Thornhill asked Mr. Thornhill.

"Wait? Why?" Mary-Larkin said. "I thought you all were the two world beaters at integration? What's the matter?" She looked from her mother, to her father, who was looking out the window, thinking hard.

After a minute, he turned to his wife and said, "No, of course not." To Mary-Larkin, he said, "Tell them to come on. If they want to come to supper, we'd better make reservations. The ladies in the circles get upset at surprise people for dinner."

"Are you sure, David?" Mrs. Thornhill said.

"What is going on?" Mary-Larkin said. "I know something's the matter."

"We'd better talk about it, Janie," Mr. Thornhill said. "Some of our church members are upset, Mary-Larkin, about Jimmi-Jo coming to choir and about our work at Wheatley and our attitude toward black people. I'm hoping, though, that we can proceed without a confrontation."

Mary-Larkin was astonished.

"It just seems too bad that several more of your friends from Wheatley should want to come now, just as the issue is coming to a head. . . ." Mrs. Thornhill said.

"Well, for heaven's sake, Mama, you're the one that wanted me to go to Wheatley so bad."

"We can't turn children away from the church or its choirs," Mr. Thornhill said.

"Of course we can't turn them away," Mrs. Thornhill said. "You're right. And you're right, Mary-Larkin. You go to Wheatley and these are your friends. We can't calculate." She paused. "We'll just do what's right."

"Well, shall I tell them to come for supper?"

Mr. Thornhill nodded. "Tell them to come for supper. Just let me know how many by Tuesday noon, so I can make the reservations."

Chapter 20

The next Wednesday Jimmi-Jo came home with Mary-Larkin, and Vanella and Augusta walked down for supper at the church and choir practice.

Reaction was swift.

Mary-Larkin learned from her mother that the worship committee, the committee of the Session that is in charge of worship services, held a stormy meeting and voted five to four to adopt a rule that only members of the church could sing in its choir.

The rule would have to be approved by the Session, the ruling body of the church. The Session was scheduled to meet the next Wednesday night.

If the rule were adopted, it would mean, of course, that Jimmi-Jo and Vanella and Augusta could not sing in the Youth Choir.

"Unless they join," Mary-Larkin pointed out.

The action of the worship committee was a shock to Mr. and Mrs. Thornhill.

"I never dreamed they'd do such a thing," Mrs. Thornhill said when she told Mary-Larkin about it.

Mrs. Thornhill abandoned her current writing project and spent all her time in the kitchen, baking like a madwoman. She made German chocolate cakes, yeast rolls, brownies, Tollhouse cookies, coconut cakes and, of course, ice-box cookies.

There was an air of crisis around the manse. Mary-Larkin had the sense of approaching battle, and she felt that people were choosing up sides.

The phone rang constantly. Some people offered their support, and others called to say—regretfully or resentfully or contemptuously, depending on the person—that they agreed with the action of the worship committee.

At her piano lesson, Mr. Maloney assured her that the worship committee was a bunch of old fogeys. "They're nothing but a group of retired Confederate generals," he said. "Don't they know the world is changing? How can they turn children away from the church? Jesus said, 'Suffer little children to come unto me.' It couldn't be clearer. . . ."

Mary-Larkin agreed with him, but she thought that life had certainly gotten even more complicated lately.

Critter's mother and father came by the manse together. Mary-Larkin felt that they were coming "as a group," in a formal way. They asked to see both Mr. Thornhill and Mrs. Thornhill. They said they'd heard about the worship committee and they offered their help and sympathy in the crisis facing Mr. Thornhill and his congregation. They offered to leave the Unitarian church and join the Presbyterian church if it would help Mr. Thornhill.

Mr. Thornhill, sincerely touched, thanked them, but

said he thought they should stay in the Unitarian church, where they felt more at home with the doctrine.

Mr. McLeod, the Youth Choir director, called up and said the music staff of the church was outraged by the action of the worship committee and wanted to resign in a body if that would help.

Mr. Thornhill told him that mass resignations were not called for—yet. "We may not have to resign," he pointed out.

"Oh," said Mr. McLeod. "So it may come to that?"

Mary-Larkin came downstairs on Saturday morning to find her mother with a cookbook open and the kitchen in chaos.

"What are you making now?" Mary-Larkin said.

"Sacher torte," Mrs. Thornhill said.

"Good gracious," Mary-Larkin said. "What else have you made? The kitchen is a mess."

"A jelly roll and some homemade hamburger buns."

"Carbohydrates for crisis—still," Mary-Larkin said, eating a homemade cinnamon roll. "Where's Papa?"

"He's in his study—at the church," Mrs. Thornhill said. "Praying."

"What's the latest?" Mary-Larkin said.

Mrs. Thornhill abandoned her cookbook and sat at the table with Mary-Larkin. "He's talked to the members of the worship committee, and the five that voted for the rule are absolutely adamant. They're upset about the integration of the schools, and now they don't want to see the Youth Choir integrated, too."

"Mama, how can they say that and be Christian?" Mary-Larkin said. "I don't understand."

"Christians see things differently," Mrs. Thornhill said. "There wouldn't be all these denominations if they didn't. Look at religious wars; look at Ireland! And the five people on the worship committee are good people. That's what makes it sad. Mrs. Phillips is one of them, and Mrs. Phillips is a wonderful woman. She honestly fears the mongrelization of the white race. She honestly believes it's God's will that the races stay separated. And Mrs. Phillips and her husband sent their maid's four children through college, paid for everything. At Tuskegee, to a black college, but they sent them. They're not bad. It's so sad, Mary-Larkin." And Mrs. Thornhill began to cry.

Mary-Larkin was aghast. "Mama!" She couldn't swallow any more cinnamon rolls. Three would have to do. "Mama, please don't cry!"

Mrs. Thornhill wiped her eyes. "I know. But I feel so sorry for your father! He *hates* confrontation. He *hates* dissension."

"What's he going to do?"

"He's trying to decide," Mrs. Thornhill said.

"Who else is on the worship committee?" Mary-Larkin asked.

"Oh, Mr. Knox—"

"Is that Sarah's father?"

"Yes, but don't be mad at Sarah, Mary-Larkin. I try not to be mad at Mr. Knox, but I can't help it. I AM MAD AT MR. KNOX! He ought to know better. It's such a hypocritical rule, anyway. The church has *paid* people that aren't members to sing in the choir when they wanted special soloists. That rule is awful. It's sinful."

125

Mary-Larkin had never seen her mother so upset.

"It's so hard on your father," Mrs. Thornhill said. "He's no radical. He's a very conservative man. He just happens to believe in the Brotherhood of Man!" Mrs. Thornhill picked up the cookbook and began to study it.

Mary-Larkin stared at her. What could she do to help? A girl of twelve, what could she do? She got up and went around and put her arms around her mother. "Mama, I love you," she said.

Mrs. Thornhill patted Mary-Larkin's arm. "And I love you," she said.

Mr. Thornhill came into the kitchen, and Mrs. Thornhill looked up at him.

"Have you decided what to do?" she said.

"Yes," he said. "I've decided that I'll tell the Session, if they approve this action of the worship committee, I'll have to resign. There's nothing else to do. I've thought about it and prayed about it for days."

"Of course, there's nothing else to do," Mrs. Thornhill said. She got up and ran around the table and they hugged each other. Mary-Larkin's eyes felt wet, and her stomach fluttered. She felt the way, almost, she had the day Ngoma had looked her in the eyes and called her "Sister." "I know you have to say that. You are absolutely right."

"It will be all right. The Lord will provide, you know that."

"I know," Mrs. Thornhill said. "We won't go hungry, but it's so sad, too. I *like* this church."

"I love this church," Mr. Thornhill said. "I wouldn't have minded staying here all my life. But there comes a time you have to take a stand, like Abraham and Isaac."

"You mean we might have to move?" Mary-Larkin said. "Unless there's a ram in the bush?"

"Yes, we might have to move," Mrs. Thornhill said sadly.

"Leave Stonewall?"

"We don't know," Mrs. Thornhill said.

"If we lived in Stonewall, but not here, I could go to Longstreet," Mary-Larkin said. She thought about it: Longstreet, with Missy and Noble. No more Wheatley, with its dull classes and Major always borrowing notepaper and Critter and Jimmi-Jo and Vanella. She'd never see Lanett's baby. Somehow it didn't seem such a glorious prospect.

Mr. Thornhill kissed his wife, ate a bite of cinnamon roll, and drank part of a cup of coffee, and then said he was going over to the church to get his secretary to call the elders and call an extraordinary Session meeting that very night, Saturday.

"I don't want it to drag on," Mr. Thornhill said. "I want those children to be welcome if they come on Wednesday—or for it to be all over."

"Papa," said Mary-Larkin.

"What is it?" he asked. "My mind's made up."

"I wasn't going to try to change your mind, Papa," she said, dismayed. "I think you're right, absolutely right. And if worse comes to worst, I'll help save money by giving up my piano lessons."

"Mary-Larkin, I thank you for your splendid spirit of sacrifice," Mr. Thornhill said. He laughed and kissed Mary-Larkin.

127

That night before supper, Mr. Thornhill called the family together for prayers. "Well, none of you children were up for morning prayers," he said, when Mary-Larkin and Joe and Luke objected. "You shouldn't mind too much."

He read the story of the Good Samaritan and prayed for God's wisdom and guidance and love. He thanked God for his loyal family, and said amen.

Mary-Larkin was oddly moved. Was this what heroes were like at home? Did all heroes *pray* all the time?

After supper, Mr. Thornhill went to the church for the Session meeting. Joe and Luke went to watch television, and Mary-Larkin and her mother read.

Mr. Thornhill came in about 9 P.M. He came in the library looking pale and tired—but smiling.

"What happened?"

"It's all over," he said. "They voted down the worship committee's rule."

"That's wonderful!" Mrs. Thornhill said. "Oh, David! How did it happen?"

"Have you got any coffee?" he asked.

"I'll make some," Mrs. Thornhill said. They all went in the kitchen and Mr. Thornhill told them about the meeting while the water boiled and the coffee dripped.

"Well, I told them they knew why the meeting had been called, and that at first I had thought I'd just let it go through in the ordinary way and then I realized I couldn't do that, that I had to take a stand, that I had to let them know that if they voted to approve the rule, I'd have to resign. I'd have no choice if the church voted to exclude people in that way."

He took a sip of the coffee his wife poured him. "And then Barney Blake made the report for the worship committee. He's the chairman and he was against the rule, but he made a very fair presentation. The discussion was pretty calm. Everybody spoke his mind without rancor. When it was time to vote, the vote was very firm and solid against the worship committee. Everybody seemed to feel that we had no choice, that you can't turn God's children from God's house, no matter who they are."

"Then it's all settled?" Mary-Larkin said. "We're going to stay here?"

"For a while, anyway," Mr. Thornhill said.

Mrs. Thornhill looked at him inquiringly. "Oh, I see," she said. "These things are never really settled, are they?"

"No, and this isn't really over. We'll lose some members over it," Mr. Thornhill said. "Van Knox said he'd have to leave the church."

"Sarah's father?" Mary-Larkin asked.

Mr. Thornhill nodded.

"Who else will leave?"

"We shouldn't talk any more about that," Mr. Thornhill said. "That's speculation at this point. Let's wait and let the Holy Spirit do its work."

Mary-Larkin went upstairs. Right had triumphed. Jimmi-Jo and the others could sing in the choir, and she'd go to Wheatley.

What if all her friends' parents left the church? What if she never saw Missy or Callie or Sarah at all?

Chapter 21

Mary-Larkin had learned already that life goes on, even after the worst crises, and after the big Session meeting, life went on. The girls from Wheatley came to choir practice regularly and sang on Sunday morning. Jimmi-Jo and Vanella even began to stay for Sunday school. They didn't much enjoy Sunday school, but they loved the choir.

And very soon, school was out for Christmas and the Gadabouts' dance was the first night of the Christmas holidays.

Mary-Larkin was excited the night of the dance.

"It's like in books," she told her mother. "My first dance."

"Most people have a terrible time at their first dance," Mrs. Thornhill said. "I was miserable."

"Why?"

"I was the only girl there in a short dress," Mrs. Thornhill said. "It was back during the depression and my mother didn't believe in frivolous things, even if there hadn't been a depression. She said it was silly for a twelve-year-old girl to have an evening dress. So I wore a short dress, and I never will forget how I felt when I walked in and everybody there had on long dresses. I sat down on an ottoman and covered up as much of my legs as I could with my skirt. I wouldn't stand up all night. I didn't dance once."

"Oh, Mama!"

"I know it was silly, but that's the way I was," Mrs. Thornhill said. She sighed.

"Well, I have a new long dress, and I know I won't be the only one in a long dress, so I won't have that problem," Mary-Larkin said. "I wish my hair were straight," she added.

"I used to want my hair to be curly," Mrs. Thornhill said. "Did you ask Critter to the dance?"

"No, ma'am. I asked Noble Paget. I don't suppose Critter is invited."

Mary-Larkin continued to feel that flutter of excitement, the sense of things, romantic and meaningful, about to happen. She loved walking up to the double doors of the country club, having the doorman open the door, and sailing through with Missy and Sarah and Denise.

They checked their wraps and walked into the ballroom, where all the boys were gathered at one end and all the girls clustered together at the other.

The refreshment table had a big silver epergne full of camellias, and magnolia leaves were massed in the urns at the edge of the stage. Mary-Larkin thought it looked lovely.

The group was getting ready on the stage, their electronic instruments making wheezing and groaning sounds, and Mary-Larkin shivered as she joined the girls.

The girls twittered. "What a pretty dress!" they all said as Mary-Larkin joined them. "What a pretty dress!" they said to Missy and Denise and Sarah. Everybody admired everybody else's dress.

Mary-Larkin realized she really didn't know many people.

She stood a little apart, looking around at the gleaming dance floor, the table with the white cloth and polished silver, the boys in their white shirts and blue blazers, at the orchestra on stage and the girls with their long, fair, straight hair, their white faces, their pretty, expensive dresses, and she felt uneasy.

Am I turning black? she asked herself. I don't seem to feel at home with white people any more.

Then the music began and Missy was dancing with Monk Stevens, and a few other couples joined them on the floor.

Noble Paget came over and asked her to dance. They danced. She had never mentioned Wheatley to him, and she did not now. When the dance was over he took her back to the girls' side of the ballroom and she talked to a girl whose name she wasn't sure of.

Both girls chatted with great vivacity; each wanted desperately for a boy to come ask her to dance but they had to talk with all this excitement to hide their dismay at not dancing.

Then the girl Mary-Larkin was talking to went off to dance with a boy Mary-Larkin had never seen before and Mary-Larkin stood by herself for a minute. Callie looked at her and turned away. Stung, Mary-Larkin moved over toward the punch table where boys and girls both gathered.

Mary-Larkin noticed a boy whose shirttail was coming out of his pants.

It's Critter! she thought, and was astonished at how glad she was to see him.

But the boy wasn't Critter at all.

Mary-Larkin talked to Sarah a while and to Grace Will Byrd, whom she hadn't seen in months. Then Bruce Davenport came to ask her to dance.

From that point on, she danced enough to feel at least decent. But she was glad when the dance was over. Very glad.

She couldn't even pretend to have enjoyed it when she was on the way home with Missy's father driving them. Missy and Sarah and Denise chattered excitedly about the marvelous time they'd had.

"Clyde danced every slow dance with me!" Sarah sighed. "It was heaven."

It wasn't much after eleven o'clock when she got home, but she felt as though she'd been up all night.

She lay awake in bed and thought, So that's a dance? So that's teenage romance? Bah.

The first week of Christmas holidays, Mary-Larkin felt curiously bereft and lonely. There was no choir practice, so she didn't see Jimmi-Jo or Vanella. She didn't see Critter. She did see Missy and some other kids from Sunday school at the young people's roller-skating party the church sponsored. She heard that Callie had a fondue party, but she didn't invite Mary-Larkin.

Two days before Christmas, Critter Kingsley appeared at her front door.

"Hello," said Mary-Larkin. "Come in." She thought he must have brought a message to her parents, or somethings.

Critter's sweater had a hole in it. He came in and said, "Do you have any popcorn?"

"I think so," Mary-Larkin said. Had he come to borrow some popcorn?

"When I was in third grade, it used to rain every Friday afternoon and I'd make popcorn and watch a Godzilla movie," Critter said. "My life has been downhill ever since."

Mary-Larkin laughed. She realized Critter had come to see her. He was funny and nice. She forgot that she'd ever regarded him as funny, in an entirely different way, and gross.

They went to the kitchen and found the popcorn.

Chapter 22

The holidays were over. Mary-Larkin had spent the second half of them having a delightful time. She and Critter had popped tons of popcorn and watched movies on television and gone roller skating and gone out to the Kingsleys' farm a couple of times to ride horseback.

Soon after school started up again, there was a seventh-grade assembly. Mr. Searle spoke to them about manners, and urged them to be polite and on time and bring pencils and notebooks to school.

Then there were the announcements about upcoming events . . . a trip to a film festival for the filmmaking class, a trip to the Distributive Education convention for the D.E. Club, a forthcoming visit to Wheatley by a black drama group . . . the beginning of an after-school drama group for students who were interested.

And then there were some mid-year awards. The seventh-grade football players got their athletic letters, small W's to be worn on sweaters or jackets. Mary-Larkin clapped hard for Critter when he got his letter, and she noticed that Critter got lots of applause.

Critter's popular, she thought. I wish I could learn from him how to make real friends. . . .

Prizes were given to winners in the essay contest on jury duty.

Then Mr. Searle said he had an unusual prize to announce. "You remember when Ngoma Odell was here?" he said. "Well, he took some of the poems some students wrote and sent them to a national poetry contest, and one of the winners came from Phyllis Wheatley Junior High School."

There was a gasp of admiration from the audience.

"It was an honorable mention—" Here, a sigh of disappointment went up from the audience. "Look," he said, "an honorable mention in a national contest is first-rate! Think of the thousands of students from all over the country that entered this contest, students in big, rich high schools!

"The winner from Wheatley is a seventh grader, Mary-Larkin Thornhill. Come up here, Mary-Larkin."

Mary-Larkin was frozen. She had completely forgotten that Ngoma Odell was going to enter Wheatley poems in the contest.

And to win a national poetry contest—even if it was only honorable mention—was incredible, a wonderful, marvelous event to be dreamed about and longed for. It was astonishing.

The kids around her were telling her to go on up on the stage, to get up and go. She sat in her chair, too frightened to move.

For now she remembered the only other time she'd been on stage at Wheatley, when she'd tried out for cheerleader and nobody had clapped and someone had hissed at her.

No, she would not go up on the stage.

"Go on, Mary-Larkin," Jimmi-Jo was saying to her. "Go on."

"I can't," Mary-Larkin said.

She felt hands behind her, reaching under her armpits and lifting her up. She looked around and it was Major, grinning hugely, who was lifting her bodily. She stood up shakily and climbed over knees to get to the aisle.

The aisle seemed two miles long, and the steps to the stage were like a cliff that had to be scaled. Her legs didn't seem to be working properly. But Mr. Searle was standing there, grinning, holding out a certificate. He came toward her and took her arm.

He got her to the center of the stage and gave her the certificate and shook her hand.

And then there was applause for her. Genuine, warm applause. Mary-Larkin turned and grinned at her fellow students in the auditorium.

She ducked her head shyly and started down the steps. The applause was dying out.

It hadn't been the kind of thunderous ovation a ninth-grade football star would get, or the kind that the most popular girl in school got when she was elected Homecoming Queen, but it had had a nice, solid sound to it.

And there had been no hisses for Mary-Larkin, no hisses for the honky this time.

It had been a long four months at Phyllis Wheatley.